at face value

For A, N, S, E, A—again, always, forever.

Emily Franklin

at face value

flux™
Woodbury, Minnesota

First Edition
First Printing, 2008

Book design by Steffani Sawyer
Cover design by Ellen Dahl
Cover image © 2008 Photodisc/SuperStock

Flux, an imprint of Llewellyn Publications

Library of Congress Cataloging-in-Publication Data

Franklin, Emily.
  At face value / Emily Franklin.—1st ed.
      p. cm.
  Summary: In this modern twist on the Cyrano story, talented and witty Cyrie Bergerac, a high school senior cursed with an enormous nose, has a secret crush on her popular friend Eddie Roxanninoff.
  ISBN 978-0-7387-1307-6
  [1. Beauty, Personal—Fiction. 2. Love—Fiction. 3. Friendship—Fiction. 4. High schools—Fiction. 5. Schools—Fiction.] I. Title.
  PZ7.F8583At 2008
  [Fic]—dc22

                                                                    2008017550

Flux
Llewellyn Publications
A Division of Llewellyn Worldwide, Ltd.
2143 Wooddale Drive, Dept. 978-0-7387-1307-6
Woodbury, Minnesota 55125-2989, U.S.A.
www.fluxnow.com

Printed in the United States of America

Acknowledgments

Thank you to Faye Bender, Andrew Karre, Heather Swain, and my family, especially my brothers, who reminded me not to be afraid of worms.

Also by Emily Franklin

For young adults

The Principles of Love (series)
> *The Principles of Love*
> *Piece, Love, & Happiness*
> *Love from London*
> *All You Need Is Love*
> *Summer of Love*
> *Labor of Love*
> *Lessons in Love*

Chalet Girls (series)
> *Chalet Girls: Balancing Acts*
> *Chalet Girls: Slippery Slopes*
> *Chalet Girls: Off the Trails*

The Other Half of Me

The Half-Life of Planets

For adults

The Girls' Almanac

Liner Notes

*Too Many Cooks: A Mother's Memoir of Tasting,
Testing, and Discovery in the Kitchen*

How to Spell Chanukah: 18 Writers Celebrate 8 Nights of Lights

Before: Short Stories about Pregnancy from Our Top Writers

It's a Wonderful Lie: 26 Truths about Life in Your 20s

one

Maybe it's your hips, how they never seem to fit into those jeans the way you wish they would. Or maybe your eyes are lopsided, just enough for you—and Steven Minsker in ninth grade—to notice. Or your coarse hair won't gather a lustrous sheen no matter how much conditioner and pomade you slather on it. Everyone has something even if they won't admit it, something about their physical being that bothers them. Myself included. You'd think that as a senior at Weston High I'd finally be over it—and maybe I am, kind of. But do you ever *really* completely get past your big butt, your ears that stick way out, your—

Wait.

In baby pictures, you can't tell. I still look cute, proportional in my green and yellow striped footie pajamas. Mom and Dad are in the background—you can just see Mom's ugly-duckling slippers (um, foreshadowing, anyone?) and one of Dad's enormous hands. He's tall, six feet seven inches, the kind of tall that always elicits stares. Mom always told me I'd be statuesque, too, but I'm totally average at five foot five.

In toddler pictures, my hair is so blonde it's white, and you still can't tell. The thing that will become my defining characteristic has not taken over, has not dominated my world.

Yet.

Then, fifth grade. Wait—backtrack. In fourth grade, I had about ten minutes of huge popularity when Daniel Simkins decided he liked me and made his intentions known on the playground (in other words, he pushed me into the muddy patch under the tire swing and told me he hated me, which resulted in a chorus of approval from the other boys and a love note from Daniel's sidekick, Robert, in my cubby). Ah, fourth grade. The total extent of my glory days.

But back to fifth grade, the year everything changed. You know those school pictures that come in a stunning variety of sizes, perfect for wallets, desktops, Grandma's piano, Mom's office, the attic, and so on? In fifth grade, my parents buckled and finally ordered the mega-set. Ninety-two photographs of me ranging from thumbnail sized for the locket no one owns to the convenient 3x5 size, bypassing the large enough 8x10 and going all the way up to the enormous 12x18, requiring custom framing.

Up until fifth grade, Dad's frugality always made them choose the standard package, two of each "Regular Size" (a phrase I wish could be my personal mantra), and that was plenty. But in a fit of parental sentimentality and an odd request from each grandparent for a new photo of me, they heaved up the extra money and went for it.

In the picture, my shirt is plain—Starbucks green, like my eyes—and my hair is long, draped carefully over my shoulders in the very self-conscious, fifth-grade way. I'm sitting with my shoulders back, as instructed by the photographer. I should have known something was wrong by the way he told me first to turn left, then to angle my head down and look up, then sighed and shot me face-on. Clearly I was not a candidate for that fake mist technique that causes an extra image of you to hover like an angel—those were only offered to the class beauties.

When we got the pictures back they were in thick manila envelopes taped to the blackboard. I pulled the one marked Cyrie Bergerac off and looked inside. Staring back at me was a shocking image: not so much a fifth grade face, but just a giant, huge, goofily large thing. My nose.

You've seen big noses, no doubt. Been at the mall and thought *wow—that's quite a honker*. But you haven't seen me. I mean that both ways—you've never seen a nose as big as mine and, if you had, you wouldn't have seen me. Because what I've found, in the seven years since those fall pictures were taken, is that no one sees past the thing they notice first.

We have tons of those pictures left over. Sure, grandparents wanted one, and my parents—blind in their love—framed the enormous one and hung it over the mantle until, in seventh grade, Wendy Von Schmedler's taunts got to me and I asked my mom and dad to remove it. Now it's in the attic somewhere—my fifth grade, canoe-nosed self stashed away with old toys and faded fashions I wish I could forget. Of course, everyone has their awkward stage, their year or two labeled with words like *gawky, chubby, lanky, high-pitched, bean pole, just a phase*.

Except my awkward stage has stuck with me.

Easy solution: get a nose job. Everyone does it, right? Everyone who has parents that let them. My "love yourself," post-hippie parents (who are totally "love and help everyone" except when they watch me play tennis, at which point they become every bit as ruthless as I am) are appalled that I would even consider changing my "natural beauty." I've tried every possible angle to get them to see my point of view, but for every point I come up with, they have a counterpoint (that comes with the territory when you have a lawyer as a father).

My point: "Dad, do you know how many girls at school have their noses fixed?"

His point: "So now you want to be just like everyone else?

And what's with the word *fixed*—it's like you girls treat your bodies like cars." Before he could start in on loving my dents and dings, or some fender analogy, I left the room.

My point: "It's considered a *minor* procedure. And it would totally help my self-esteem."

Their point: "First of all, doctors call things *procedures* to make people feel more comfortable about what's really an *operation*. The fact is, a nose job is elective surgery—and we don't agree with it."

My counterpoint: "What if I needed to, like for reconstruction or something?"

Their point (#4,532): "That would be different."

Me: "So basically, I should hope that I get clunked in the face with a tree limb or something . . . "

Their response (shaking heads): "You have so much going for you—good grades, editor of the paper, natural blonde hair in society obsessed with hair color . . . "

And lastly . . .

My Point: "But Mom, you highlight your hair—that's not *natural*."

Rebuttal: "I only started that three years ago after the grays started taking over my head—I feel younger inside than I look outside." Dad gives her hand a squeeze for moral (and follicular) support.

My second point: "Well, I feel prettier on the inside than I do on the outside."

I felt so lame for saying that out loud, partly because it's a lie, that I retreated to the bathroom for an extra-long shower. I like to sit on the floor of the shower and let the water rain onto me like I just happen to be caught in a storm (of course, one would hope if I were caught outside in a storm that I wouldn't be naked—but I overlook that little factoid).

The result of all this rhinoplasty back-and-forth is that, since I'm a minor and they won't sign the consent forms, I made an appointment at Dr. Singer's in town for the first open slot after my eighteenth birthday (I was born at 12:02 a.m. on January 1). Since he's a friend of the family, I'm allowed to go in this fall for pre-op consults. I figure I can always change my mind . . . but at this point, I'm expecting that day to change my life.

two

I keep a reminder—a tiny remnant of my fifth grade discovery that I will never be the kind of girl people instantly (or ever) crush on—pasted in my journal: one of the tiny, thumbnail-size pictures from that year.

And it's this miniscule image of myself, complete with bird's perch nose, that I'm staring at when Eddie Roxanninoff gets up on stage in front of the whole school to make his plea for SBP (student body president). I flip my journal closed, concealing the picture, and look around. Eddie takes a seat next to the other candidates, on one of the wooden chairs at the side of the stage, and waits calmly for the assembly to begin.

Clusters of sophomore girls sit off to the left, drooling at the senior guys who sit way at the back of the auditorium feeling as though they've earned their place there, and juniors are sprinkled to the right. Even though I'm a senior and have trudged through the first three years of high school like everyone else, I'm not coveting a back row spot. Since I'm covering the event for the *Weston Word* (is it possible that something as seemingly tame as a school election warrants a two-page article in the school paper?), I have to sit up at the front like it's a presidential press conference.

I have a habit of putting my feet up on the seat in front of me—a big auditorium faux pas—and Mrs. Cutler makes it clear with a cough that this is most unacceptable. I put my boot-clad feet on the floor and sit up, trying to make some notes for the article. With my right elbow balancing on the armrest and my notebook on my lap, I try to list all the other class-president nominees in the order they're seated on stage. Except, as I lean forward to see them, the notebook slides off my lap and my papers scatter all over the less-than-clean auditorium floor.

"Do you want me to help you?" Leyla Christianson asks, immediately leaning down to collect my fallen pages.

"Thanks," I say and try to shake off my klutziness. Not because I care that I dropped my notebook, but because anything that brings attention to me usually results in someone making a crack at my expense—and ends with me flattening the insult-thrower with a cutting remark.

I look behind me. I'm in luck today, since Wendy Von Schmedler and her popular cronies are settled at the back, the freshmen are too new to risk insulting a senior, and the sophomores are too busy trying to look cool to notice me—or rather, to notice my nose. But I'm not interested in the general audience. I'm here for one reason and one reason only.

Crushes start like insect bites. Hardly there at first, then a sharp sting, and then the absolute need to deal with the itch. I'm about to indulge in some serious scratching when my reverie is broken by—

"Can you move, please? We want to sit here with Leyla." This to me from Wendy Von Schmedler, who has brought her Xeroxed minions with her. Each girl is trying to stand with a hip cocked to one side, Wendy's trademark pose from seventh grade when she tripped me in the back stairwell and I fell onto my face. The blood stains never came out of my white sweater.

Maybe I should move to another seat. I could. But I don't, because—

"Actually, Wendy, I need to sit here." I pat my notebook as if this will inform her of why (the paper, the article, facts and figures). I can feel a swirl of words brewing inside my head, waiting for the slightest provocation to be spewed all over Wendy's made-up face.

Wendy does the combination hair-toss-with-shoulder-shrug to signal to her troops that a situation is starting. No one is supposed to mess with the Schmedler. "And the reason you need to sit here is … " I open my mouth to answer while I'm still calm, but she side-checks me: " … because you adore the smell of old stage sweat and you know that this—" she gestures to my body part in question "—will suck up any scent?" A couple girls near her giggle, and Wendy grins, giving me a look that somehow mixes contempt with pity.

Give me insults, but don't feel bad for me. Inside, the anger boils. "You know what?" I say. "You'd be better off doing the insult in another way."

Wendy looks confused. I've found that if you react to meanness, you're doomed. More insults will fly right at you. But you can really get to people by slapping them with their own missteps. They suffer, and you can revel in their pathetic attempts at a comeback.

I cross my arms over my chest and offer, "Why not stress the size of my nose and say 'Hey, Cyrie, you can afford to sit at the back. Your schnoz can certainly pick up scents from miles away.'" Cue laughter from Wendy's minions until she shoots them a look.

"Fine." Wendy nods. "You've got a point. So move—go sit where no one has to look at you." She thumbs to the back of the auditorium. "We want to sit here," she says again. Her crew—known in my mind at the PBVs (pretty but vapids)—wait expectantly.

But I continue talking as though she hasn't said a word. Around us, people settling into their seats begin to listen. "The thing is, Wendy, you *want* to be able to deliver clever slander, but the truth is, you lack the brain power to finesse the defamation."

"Big word, big word, blah blah blah." She cocks her hip so far out I worry she'll topple onto my lap.

I stand up so that we're face to face, nearly nose to nose. "Exactly. Blah blah blah. That's you in a nutshell." Leyla tries to pull me back down, to settle my rising emotions, but it doesn't work. I don't raise my voice, but try instead to keep my face steely and focused right on Wendy's. "Someday, I'll look back on this day and it'll be just another day when some pathetic attempt at viciousness tried to do the obvious thing and point out that my nose is, in fact, large." Wendy's half-smile fades as I go on. "I've had lots of days like this. Yep, it's big." I touch my nose, grabbing it with my whole palm for a good show as more students watch the interchange. "But you'll look back on this day and realize that no matter what happens, you'll always be this shell of a person. Half bitchy and half…" I pause for dramatic effect. "Nothing."

Wendy swallows so big that it's audible. Her discomfort echoes through the room. Then her hip finds its way back to a normal position, and, wordlessly, she swivels with her group and herds them back to the back of the auditorium, where the cool crowd can gossip without the principal's wrath.

I sit back down in my seat, my heart thumping, satisfaction spreading through me like butter on warm toast. I flip through my notebook, pretending not to notice the people in the surrounding rows and the words they utter. "Harsh." "But true." "But too cruel." At first I think they're talking about Wendy, but they're not.

After she clears her throat, Leyla finally speaks. "Remind me never to pick on you."

I want to explain, to open my lips and justify the mini-slaying to Leyla, but I don't. Wendy started it. I was just defending myself. She's the mean one. Fight fire with fire. Mess with the bull, you get the horns. I shake my head at myself, realizing I've just referred to myself as the bull: a giant lumbering animal everyone wants to avoid.

"You look nice today," Leyla says, breaking the tension. She feels the thin merino wool of my pine-green sweater. "That color really brings out your eyes."

"You mean it takes away from my nose?" I say, trying to downplay the prior scene.

"I never..." Leyla catches my grin. "Oh—you're kidding. I get it."

Leyla Christianson. Her classic rock name can't disguise her plight as a more-than-slightly tongue-tied member of the *Weston Word* staff, interviewed and "hired" last year (though we don't pay, our high school paper is the second-best in the state, so we have standards that would make *The New York Times* proud) by none other than myself. Even though I'd balked at the idea of having one of the PBVs on staff, having Leyla around has been better than I expected. Once she joined, she semi-retired from PBV status, and—not coincidentally—became my friend.

Leyla was a member of that group that exists at every high school—the ruling class. There are different factions of it: the nicer girls, the bitchy ones, and then the über-pretty but mentally vacated ones (the ones who can spend an entire forty-five-minute lunch block discussing the textures of gloss versus lipstick, but can't seem to muster one intelligent thought in World Politics or American Civilization or even Home Ec—how hard is it not to singe the turkey meatloaf beyond recognition?). Now Leyla treads the precarious line of half-in, half-out of Wendy Von Schmedler's crowd. Sometimes I can tell she feels split, trying to manage the balance between me (and the *Word*) and the PBVs.

But despite her swag of perfect hair (light brown with natural strands of gold woven through, with a sheen so high it's like she has those model reflectors on her at all times), despite her tall-but-not-so-tall-as-to-scare-off-potential-suitors body, despite her C-cup breasts and sweet smile, Leyla is not entirely vapid. She just doesn't believe it yet.

I turn to her in the now slightly stuffy auditorium. "Do you mind covering the second speaker?"

I've been trying to practice delegating some of the writing responsibilities. Even though I'm the editor, I'm not supposed to do all the work—but it's difficult for me to back off. I admit that I'm way too involved with all aspects of the *Word*, but it's been kind of my pet project since I convinced Mr. Reynolds, the faculty manager, that I should be able to join as an eighth grader oh so many years ago. Territorialism is what you could call it. Kind of the way you feel when you notice a new band first, when you claim their single as yours, only to find two weeks later that the cheerleading squad has chosen it for their fall bus anthem. Maybe it's just me, but sometimes I feel like *finders keepers* should apply to all things. People, too.

"Sure," Leyla says. "But I don't have my books with me. And before you get annoyed, it's a hard habit to break."

Leyla has a reputation for forgetting her books, her bag, a pencil, her debate notes, her jacket in a blizzard, and so on. Then she pauses and looks at me. I lean in and we sing, way off tune, a couple of lines from "Hard Habit to Break," a cheesy old Chicago song my mom had as the theme to her junior prom. Like me, Leyla is always downloading songs and making mixes, and—to her credit—she knows a lot of cool tunes. Her love of music was what first made me look past her "somewhat dim" reputation and get to know her for the person she is under her teen magazine exterior.

I hand Leyla a couple of pieces of paper and a pen from Any Time Now (my favorite place for coffee, dessert, or just sitting in the town center).

"I'm not writing," she says, and her voice goes up an octave.

"Don't panic," I tell her. "I'm not saying you have to write the article—just take notes for me."

Leyla breathes hard and bites her lip, thinking. "Fine, okay. I can do that. But don't judge me on how good they are. You know I can't write."

"You can write—you just need practice," I say.

"You've read my stuff. It sucks. I just don't have a way with words. Not like you."

"Ah, flattery will get you everywhere." I smile at her. "Wait a sec—you'll need something to lean on." I search in my bag for a book. I pull out *Crime and Punishment* and hand it to her.

"I didn't know you were taking Great Novels," Leyla says and studies the front of the book. Great Novels is a senior course elective, but since I've already read most of the books, I skipped out on it.

"I'm not," I say. "I'm just reading Dostoyevsky for fun." I smile at her as she rolls her eyes.

"Yeah, some fun." She writes the date, event, and location at the top of her paper like I taught her to do. It's standard paper protocol, so you can hand in your notes with your article for the sake of fact checking. "So, you want me to write notes only about candidate number two, or all of them?"

"I've got the first one covered, but if you can detail all the rest … " I pretend to look busy, to cover my blushing. Territorialism on number one? On Eddie Roxanninoff? Maybe. But I keep quiet. "That way I can write up the event in general. Now, let me just check who the first candidate is … " My voice trails off as I flip through my notes, pretending to be searching for who is speaking first.

"You mean Rox?" Leyla says. She actually points to him on stage. The lights are bright up there and he doesn't see her, thank God.

"Right. Eddie Roxanninoff."

"Rox," Leyla says.

"Eddie," I reiterate. "I don't want to be like everyone else." I pause. That's not entirely true. "It's that … I just like calling him by his real name. Like a reporter." Hopefully, Leyla can't tell how just the thought of saying his name makes my hands shake, my heart race, my mind prone to fantasy images of us slow dancing in the moonlight (okay, I know I plagiarized that notion from any number of horribly cheesy songs, but it's just a dream).

"Fine. Be different just for the sake of it," Leyla says, and gets me at my own game. Everyone—from frosh up to faculty—calls him Rox. But I call him Eddie. I figure it's one less way to blend into the crowd, and since I already stand out, I may as well carry the theme through. "Oh. They're about to start."

The real reason I want to shrug off part of my editorial duties in this assembly is not so Leyla can practice her writing skills or hone her journalistic ability. It's totally crush-driven.

If Leyla writes about the other candidates, I can focus on Eddie's speech and Leyla can write about Dave Edison (who is not the inventor of a light bulb; more like the inventor of the Weston hook-up—but more on that later), Nicole Marchese, and Jessica Lauren Bettle (who runs for everything just so she can list it on her college applications as "potential class president").

"Yeah, make sure to write an…um…in-depth report about Dave Edison," I say, giving Leyla Dave's trademark sleazy wink-and-nod combo.

"Sure, stick me with the hook-up king. Fine." Leyla grins at me. Then she realizes something, and laughs. "Oh, wait—I did bring my book bag—I'm so proud of myself." She hands me back my book and pen and gets out her red notebook and signature pen, a ballpoint she wrapped in green silk floral tape and topped with a fake sunflower. On the one hand, it's semi-sweet. On the other hand, accessories like that don't help in her attempt to be (or to appear) less flakey.

Just as the lights dim, Jill Carnegie appears in the aisle to my left and leans over me like I don't exist, the scent of her expensive perfume wafting into my nostrils (cue a joke about how I could probably smell her two states over with the size of my nostrils), to pass on some crucial social info to Leyla.

"Hey, Leyla." Jill ignores me. "Sorry to be so … *nosey* … " She lets her dark ringlets cascade down for dramatic effect and pauses to make sure I've heard her attempted slight. "But I wanted to say hi and remind you that you have a life. It's waiting for you at the back of the auditorium, okay?" Leyla nods. "Meet us for lunch today?" This last part isn't so much a question, more a command.

Jill slithers away, her color-coordinated outfit on display as she sashays up the wide aisle without so much as a glance back at me. I'm too focused on writing my notes to deal with her "nosey" comment. Plus, it's too lame to bother with.

Leyla turns to me as the lights go out. "Sorry about Jill."

"Don't be sorry *about* her, be sorry *for* her—she gives new meaning to the word translucent."

I know that there is nothing about Jill that will last through the day, let alone make a mark on the decade or a lifetime. I flash to my own reflection. I could be one of those people who looks so different they feel the need to hide—or I could be the reverse, one of those kids who feels really different but looks average, so dresses in plaid or pierces themselves all over or, like Molly Parks, comes to school clad in a top made entirely of safety pins. (She was asked to go home and change, not so much because of the potential for skin showing but because the school nurse was concerned about pricking hazards.)

So yes, I could be that girl in the corner—and maybe part of me still is, inside. But most of the things I'm good at—tennis, editing, even writing—benefit from being around other people. For three years at Weston High, one of my saving graces was the tennis team. As a freshman I tried out for, made, and led the varsity team to victory, sophomore year was one straight win, and junior year my parents cheered me as I played in the New England High School Masters.

But this year, the start of school has not involved rackets, running court lengths, or dealing with early Wednesday dismissals for away matches. My attention has fully turned over to other activities. The only trouble is, I think that tennis served (ha—a sports pun!) as a defense, for me, against the popular set. Wendy Von Schmedler and her crew couldn't unleash their true fury because some of those girls played on the team and needed me. Now, though, all bets are off, and more and more I'm getting the sense that my defense this year will be on the home court—otherwise known as the locker-rimmed halls of Weston High.

I still carry a tennis ball in my bag and squeeze it when

I get nervous—like when I watch Eddie on stage. I turn to glance at Leyla and her note taking.

She sighs and starts writing, the sunflower pen bobbing with each letter.

"Remember not to have a bias. Just write it as it happens. You know, keep the details clear, and..." I peer over her shoulder to see what she's written so far: mainly descriptions of the stage, the seating arrangements, and her name in bubble letters. Her handwriting is neat—round and legible—an editor's dream. It's the content I'm checking.

"I know, Cyrie." Leyla nudges me off.

"Sorry." I'm a shameful snoop. That is, I snoop and feel guilty for it—with birthday gifts stashed under my parents' bed, with always wanting to know the details of conversations even when they're not mine.

Leyla tucks her hair behind her ears, and looks at me a minute before starting to write again. Sometimes I think that if we could meld, we'd make the perfect person. Her looks, my brain. Well, that, but also her way of going after what she wants and my ability to problem-solve.

Principal Richards comes onto the stage and ahems into the microphone.

"Welcome, everyone, to this year's presidential election!" I make a note about comparing the school traditions with the American government's electoral process. Students whoop and shout, faculty look half-bored, half-excited. "Our first speaker is an athlete..." (cue to the jocks to shout out for one of their own), "an A-student" (cue to the brains—if they'd look up from their books—and faculty to clap), "and a musician..." (the rockers, stoners, and every female in the audience gushes). "Give it up for our first speaker, Eddie Roxanninoff... of course, you know him better as Rox."

From this, you'd think Eddie Roxanninoff had a lock on the position of class president. And you'd think he was, without a doubt, the most popular and well-respected guy in the school. And he nearly is. But what makes him even more appealing (at least in my eyes) is that he's not. If there was ever a class popularity ranking (like what they have for academics), Eddie Roxanninoff would be in the top five, but not number one or two. (You could even have a PGPA. Suffice to say, my popularity grade point average would suck big-time. Um, 1.8 anyone?)

Basically, Eddie's just too nice to be the most popular. He's too much the guy who stops Kyle Brickman from shoving Andy Grinks into his locker just for being in the wrong place at the wrong time. Eddie's the guy who organizes trash pick-up day at the local parks and playgrounds, and makes it seem cool and fun with water balloon fights and live bands. And Eddie is the one who, when no one asked Emily Kimberly to dance at the all-school formal last winter, walked over to her and led her to the floor for the entire length of "Stairway to Heaven." He's that guy.

And the fact that he's tall (six one and a half), in incredible shape (as in plays soccer, skis, and was recruited by Oxford University in England for rowing but is not sure he's going), and one of the best-looking guys on the planet doesn't hurt, either.

Except it does hurt. A little. Okay, a lot. In that way when you really, really want something so much your whole body knows it. Or when you desire something enough that imagining having it almost makes it worse—like a reminder that you don't have it. In my case, thinking about having Eddie Roxanninoff—dating him, kissing him, having him fall in love with me—is so distant, so impossible, such a secret that gnaws at me, that watching him up there, all six foot one and a half inches of him, makes me smile and makes me want to cry, too.

In the safety of the dark auditorium, I look at the profiles of other people, the curve or flatness of their faces, their mouths open or closed while they watch Eddie give his speech. I stare at their noses—their plain, petite, crooked, rhinoplastied, average, bumpy noses—and know that, with the lights out, I can almost blend in.

three

You're in the wrong spot," Mrs. Talbot says. She nearly pinches my shoulder as she makes me move from one side of the lunch table to the other, so that I'm no longer across from Eddie Roxanninoff but next to him. The Weston High PTA, after reading about social status and student self-esteem, took it upon themselves to "restructure typical teen-age social situations." Basically, this means that at lunch and study hall, you can't sit with your friends. Supposedly, this discourages cliques and hazing, but in reality all it does is stall it.

Mrs. Talbot, study-hall hound and retro-fied Home Ec teacher, is convinced that the girls at Weston High are too brainy for our own good. She will actually say things in class that suggest it's more important for us to be able to calculate how to accurately measure for wallpaper (get the square footage of the room; for every door in the room subtract twenty-one square feet, for every window subtract fifteen square feet from the total square footage above) or make meatloaf (pound some ground meat into a pan and slosh ketchup on it) than it is to have an opinion or be able to debate.

And it's not like I'd win the championship for gray matter, but as far as grades are concerned—well, it's not a problem. But I'd be the first to tell you that it's easier to be good at something you can control, like calculus or memorizing historical facts. It's difficult to ace a major crush—nearly impossible (for me, anyway) to get an A in love.

So, I have Eddie on my left and Lizzie Driscoll to my right, some underclassman across from me, and various other students around me who span the social strata. The PTA's plan for mingling does work—to a point. It breaks up cliques, but it's not like everyone is suddenly enthralled and talking across the social barriers. Lizzie Driscoll would rather sit in silence, caressing her switched-off cell, than deign to talk to me. The only time she ever spoke to me was last year in drama class when she asked me if my nose had its own zip code. I then proceeded to inform her—and the rest of the class—that if my nose did have its own zip code, she wouldn't be able to add all the numbers up; the math would be just too tricky for her. Score another few points for me. Not that anyone's keeping count.

Eddie finishes his turkey sandwich and takes a swig from his water bottle. I polish my apple absent-mindedly on my shirt and try not to stare at Eddie's hands. His hands are—or look—soft but strong.

"What's on your mind, Cyrie? Figuring out how to cure world hunger?" Eddie asks. Then he notices my eyes glued to his hands (not literally—that would hurt). He flips his hands over for my inspection. "Still calloused." I watch as he points. "I painted houses all summer. You knew that, right? Plus rowing…" I want to comment, to say that I painted my room this summer, that I know how tiring painting is. I want to ask him about his summer job, ask him if he thinks he'll row at Oxford next year, thousands of miles away—but then I get distracted by the thought of him being so far away, and clam up.

"Sorry you didn't win class president," I say, and then wish I hadn't—he's probably had a ton of people say the same thing to him. "I'm sure you would've been great."

"Thanks," Eddie says and leans back in his seat. "It's no big deal." Then he looks at me for a few seconds without looking away. Usually when people look at me they get transfixed by my nose, and then they either refuse to look at me at all or can't stop staring at it. But Eddie looks at my eyes. "You look preoccupied, Cyrie. And I doubt it's about my lack of presidential status, crushing though it is."

I nod at him and bite my lip. "I guess I am kind of pre-occupied," I say. Lately, it's become harder and harder to deny my feelings for Eddie. It's one thing to have a crush on some-one you don't know, or admire someone from a distance, but it's entirely different when you spend a portion of every day with this person.

"Well, let me know if you want to talk about it—what-ever the preoccupation thing is, I mean." Eddie leans in just close enough to make me lose my breath, close enough that I can smell his Tom's of Maine cinnamint toothpaste. Not that I know this from, say, brushing my teeth near him. I wish. Or maybe, I don't wish—I mean, how romantic could it be to scrub and floss *a deux*? I only know these informational tidbits because the *Weston Word* does a weekly poll.

When our town got hit with a four-day-long blizzard last year and snow totals reached fifty-two inches (highlights included sledding from the low roof over the paper offices into the snow bank below), we had to dip into our lame ques-tions. So I called around to random students and asked what their preferred brand of toothpaste was. Some students hung up on me, others took the question seriously, others—like Wendy Von Schmedler and her sidekick Jill—were just so bored that they actually took the time to debate the various merits of Crest versus Colgate and so on. Of course, since I was in charge of the ridiculous poll to begin with, I figured it wouldn't hurt to call one more person. Sad but true, I know Eddie's number by heart. Not because I'm a stalker (though on my more pathetic days I see why this could appeal), but because I have the excruciating advantage (or disadvantage, depending on how you see it) of working with Eddie—love of my life so far—in not just science lab, but at the paper, too.

So that's how, when he leans in and not-quite-whispers something to me, I can recognize the cinnamon scent on his breath. In a crowded lunchroom filled with scents of salami, tuna-noodle casserole, and tomato soup, all I can smell is Eddie's toothpaste.

"Hello? Tune in, Tokyo?" Eddie asks with his eyebrows raised. "You okay, Chief?"

"Yeah, I'm fine—good. Just tired, I guess." When all else fails, you can always blame fatigue. Fatigue makes a damn good cover-up for *I'm secretly in love with you*.

Eddie snaps a fake photo of me, miming a close-up. "Girl Wakes Up in Puddle of Own Drool ... "

"Story to follow ... " I add. It's a game we play where one of us finds a totally un-newsworthy scene and we take turns making up the headline. We invented it during a colossally long science presentation on single celled organisms. The headline game has gotten us through many a boring paper meeting, but before I have the chance—

"Oh my God! I have to tell you something. Rox ... "

Lizzie Driscoll, senior class flirt, plops herself down on Eddie's lap, promptly distracting him with her perky boobs and nearly flawless face, and thus ending our brief interaction. I stand up and start to clear my tray.

Eddie is in the middle of being whispered to, but looks up from the face-to-face and nods to me. "You taking off?"

"I have to go—that story on the new path to the gym is due." Could I sound cooler? It's like I am actually missing the gene for smooth. But I'm not. I'm only missing it around him. He's wit kryptonite for me.

The final bell rings, signaling that yet another day of senior year has slid by. I'd like to head to Any Time Now, to have a misto made with organic coffee and steamed 2 percent milk, to read, snack, and people-watch—but I can't. I head instead to my second home, otherwise known as the *Weston Word* headquarters on the far side of campus, across from the gym. The office is one long rectangle broken into sections: editorial, photo, layout, and The Heap.

At the back of the rectangular room, "The Heap" is the affectionate name given long ago to the oversized table, four filing cabinets, and floor-to-ceiling bookcase, all crammed tightly with old issues of the newspaper, empty coffee mugs, pictures from 1990-something, half-used reams of paper, and other odds and ends. It's impossible to sit down without sitting on a stack of books, or shifting a bunch of papers to the floor. It's these ever-changing towers—of newspapers and yearbooks and clusters of pencils—that make The Heap a sort of moveable work of art.

Or just a pig sty. It depends on how you see it. To me, it feels homey—familiar and messy and newspaperish—like I'm the editor of a national paper or something.

"So." Mr. Reynolds, the faculty advisor for the *Word*, leans against one of the filing cabinets and calls us to order. Not like we're ever that orderly. The drawers are so full they won't close all the way, and he rests his arms on one, making his appearance even more casual than it usually is. "As you know, this year we have a new task. We've been nominated—and by 'nominated,' I mean I fought tooth and nail—to run the Annual Fall Auction for our school scholarship fund."

Leyla comes in late, and sits near me on the cluttered workbench. She looks flushed and excited, but maybe it's just the fall air. She takes a place next to Linus, my paper buddy. Linus has been at the *Word* as long as I have, but has never climbed the ranks. He's not a senior staff writer, just a plain old staff writer. He's a good writer and a capable student, well-rounded, a kind of under-the-radar sort of person. Cute, but not obvious, with straight dark hair, a slim build, and a smile he rarely reveals entirely. When he does reveal it, it totally brightens the room.

Linus and I get along well. As if he knows I'm thinking about him, he gives me a hello while Mr. Reynolds starts talking again, spelling out "Cyrie" in sign language. The *Y* reminds me of how people hold their hand to pretend to talk on the phone.

Linus' dad is deaf, and when we were freshmen, Linus spent the better part of a summer teaching me a variety of signs and the whole alphabet. Every once in a while, we sign something basic like *I'm hungry* or *this is boring* during a class or a paper meeting, but mostly Linus likes to spell stuff out to me so I can check a story idea before he asks Mr. Reynolds if he can cover it. "Basically," I said to Linus this past summer, when we went canoeing on the Connecticut River, "you use me to cover your ass. I'm like your silent sounding board." Linus agreed, shrugged, and kept paddling.

Summer feels far away now, even though August was only a few weeks ago. Time seems to fast-forward after the end of July, and by mid-August it may as well be October.

"Leslie kindly printed up the stat sheets from the last few years of auctions," Mr. Reynolds is saying. "It's a tough crowd, and a tough time of year. People are feeling pressured to buy holiday gifts…"

Noticeably absent from our auction meeting is Eddie. Just as I'm about to wonder where he could be, he appears, all apologetic. Mr. Reynolds turns his attention to him. "Rox—nice of you to join us today."

"Sorry, Mr. Reynolds. I got held up in the library…" Eddie slings his backpack onto the table and looks around for a place to sit. His green eyes crinkle on the sides when he laughs, which he does frequently, even to help avoid getting in trouble. The laugh spreads to others as fast as gossip, and pretty soon we're all chuckling for no good reason except that Eddie's just that kind of guy—good-natured and yet just a little aloof, which gives him the perfect blend of openness and mystery.

Mr. Reynolds sighs. "Look, I know you're a senior—that many of you are seniors—and you're busy with colleges and your new place in the high school hierarchy, but I expect one hundred percent from you this year." He looks at me, even though I wasn't late. "All of you."

I open my mouth to defend myself, but catch some weird glance between Leyla and Eddie. It's not the length of the look—just a quick nod—but it plants a thought in my head that I can't shake off. No matter how close I am with Leyla and or what good buddies I am with Eddie, I'm still just that girl with the big nose—not one of them, that group of good-looking Weston students who walk the halls without feeling the need to defend themselves on a daily basis. It's true that Eddie is friends with everyone (not so much enmeshed in the group as admired by it), and of course Leyla's kind of on the outskirts now. But still, I'm the one without access to that Land of the Lookers.

"So, do we have a theme for the auction?" I ask. "Or is it purely a get-the-goods, raise-the-money type of deal?"

"What kinds of themes are you thinking about?" Mr. Reynolds asks.

"What about Winter Wonderland?" Leyla suggests.

"It's a *fall* auction," I say. I try to soften my tone so it's not an insult, but Josh and the rest of the sports staff crack up. Leyla blushes and won't look at me. She and Josh went out for a year, and when they broke up he was in charge of spreading some not-particularly-nice rumors about her. "What about cornucopia?"

Steven Bundt coughs and makes some comment—probably lewd—under his breath. Mr. Reynolds rolls his eyes. "Excuse me, Steven?"

"Nothing." Steven raises his hands and shrugs to prove his innocence.

"A cornucopia," I explain. "Meaning: abundance, profusion."

"In English, Cyrie," preppy Leslie requests. She writes for our gossip section, "Word from the Word."

Eddie stands up. "I totally get it, Cyr. The fall harvest." He nods at me and smiles, and we alternate the explanation.

When I stand up, my hair falls from its loose knot, sending a wash of white-and-yellow-blonde across my shoulders as I talk. "So, you know how autumn is this time of reaping what you sow—like seeds or apples or wheat."

"We'd have, like, a visual theme," Eddie continues.

"Throw a few bales of hay and some pumpkins into the gym and we're all set."

"Forget the gym," I say and swat Eddie's arm without thinking about it, because I'm just that into this idea. "Why not try to get Wilson Farms to close down for a night and take over their barn … "

Leyla pipes up. "My uncle knows the woman who runs the Seaport Aquarium."

Silent moment. Leyla looks at me like she can't figure out what she said that inspired quiet. Eddie turns to her. "That's a cool offer, Leyla. But … um, I'm not sure if fish would tie in to the autumn theme."

"No, sure, of course." Leyla nods. "I just thought it would be an awesome place for a party."

"You're right, it would be," I say, and think how ironic it is that Leyla looks even more beautiful when she's blushing—her cheeks are sun-kissed pink, her eyes bright. Her nose, of course, is pert and perfect. "Maybe the prom committee would think about that as a place."

Leslie jumps in. "Totally—great idea, Leyla." Later, Leslie will claim the idea was her own, but right now, Leyla is just glad she wasn't ridiculed—again.

"Let's get back to the auction," Mr. Reynolds says.

I shift my weight from one foot to the other, suddenly aware that my right foot is asleep; the pins-and-needles effect is driving me crazy. "We could also have an intellectual theme of cornucopia—the abundance this community has to offer. People would contribute stuff to the auction … "

Eddie moves so he's standing next to me. I try not to flinch with joy and surprise when his thigh brushes against mine. He's in his soccer uniform, a blue shirt that brings out the blue rings in his oceany-green eyes, and yellow shorts that reveal his still-summer-brown bare legs. "And there'd be this mixing of harvesting produce, and donating items, and harvesting money for the scholarship fund."

Mr. Reynolds nods so enthusiastically that his head is in danger of coming off. Even Leslie and the other gossip writers (Gossip Girls, we call them) are happy—they envision lots of chatter and couples getting together among the scarecrows and hay.

Steven Bundt raises his hand out of habit (we don't have to raise hands at the *Word*) and Mr. Reynolds calls on him. "This sounds kind of cool, but what's really going to set this year's auction apart?"

Without missing a beat, I respond. "The theme will be a great way for us to encourage—and this is the phrase we could use—'ultimate giving.' My mom's a fundraiser and she's always telling me how the best way to ask for something is to let the other person offer."

Leyla looks at me. "But how would that work—aren't we supposed to ask them to donate?"

"Yeah, but if you use the psychology of fundraising, then it'll work better."

"This is lame," Josh from sports says. "I have to report on Coach Basker's new drills." He checks his watch against the giant clock on the wall, which is perpetually six minutes fast.

"Give Cyrie a chance," Leyla says. I grin at her, to thank her and to make up for my fall auction comment.

"Josh—your dad's got a fashion company, right?"

Josh nods, no doubt wishing his dad did something more sports-oriented. "Yeah, he's a buyer for PJ Clarkson's. Last year he got them to donate an outfit."

"PJ Clarkson's is a huge, high-end chain, so push it a bit more. See if he can get them to ask a really cool company, like Theory or something, to donate an entire wardrobe."

The fashionistas among us get excited. "I love Theory!"

"Right," I say. "And Steven, don't you go to the Bahamas every year?"

Steven nods. "Sure. Beaches, babes, beers…" He looks at Mr. Reynolds. "Just kidding about the beers. What's your point, Cyrie?"

Wordlessly, Eddie gets my okay to explain. "So, call the place you go—the hotel or private rental—and ask them if they'll give a two-week stay for a good cause."

"They'll never donate two weeks," Steven says.

"Of course not," I agree. "But the psychology of fundraising is to ask for something outrageous, that you'll never get. So then the person feels bad, and gives you something a bit less … "

"Like a free week—or weekend?"

"Exactly," Eddie and I say at the same time.

"Wendy Von Schmedler's family has a cabin on Lake Chevageaux," Leslie says. "I bet they'd go for it."

"And instead of a free bunch of helium balloons this year, we should ask Up Up and Away to donate a hot air balloon ride," Josh says.

I make a mental note to ask about a free something (lifetime coffee?) at Any Time Now, glad to have an excuse to go there. Then the meeting dissolves into a mess of ideas about which companies to pester for gift items, which individuals to ask about donating, and culminates with Mr. Reynolds making an announcement.

"Guys—everyone! I know we're excited, but listen up." He does one of those whistles with his fingers that's loud enough to stop a train. We all get quiet. "The auction is only a couple months away—so let's use our time well. Cyrie, Rox, since you two seem to work well together and you're both seniors, I think you should co-chair the event. Run everything by me, of course." He waits for our reactions.

"Sounds good," I say and smile.

"I'm game," Eddie says and licks his amazing lips.

"You two make quite a team," Mr. Reynolds says. The sports bell rings, telling us the meeting is officially adjourned.

I'm bubbling inside. Ideas are swirling and racing in my brain, and the fact that I have yet another reason to partner up with Eddie Roxanninoff makes my feet feel like they're gliding on the scummy school linoleum.

Eddie is halfway out the door when he turns to me. "I'm looking forward to working with you, Chief. Again." He pauses and snaps a fake photo of me. "Girl Wins Award for Most Creative Ideas ... "

"Story to follow," I say, and snap one of him. "Boy Wonder Helps Girl Get Her Point Across." This is my thank you to him. Not that he needs one, but I feel it shouldn't go unmentioned.

In the corridor, Eddie snaps one last fake shot of me. It's a close-up and I can see him leaning in, moving me so I'm leaning up against the wall of lockers. I can envision him giving the faux photo a headline, like *Class King Makes Unlikely Choice for Queen*, before he kisses me ...

And just as I'm relishing our imagined moment together, Leslie and her Gossip Girls go by. Eddie waves at them, the fashion crew giggles, and, worst of all, Eddie's hand—still frozen in picture snapping mode—accidentally swats me. His palm lands squarely on my nose, causing a rush of pain. A slow but steady drip of blood spatters my light blue shirt, and stains Eddie's soccer sweatshirt.

four

"Are you sure you're okay?" Eddie asks for the fifteenth time.

"I'm fine," I say and look both ways before we cross Maple Street, the main drag in town.

In front of Any Time Now, Eddie hands me my book bag, which he insisted on carrying. I take it dramatically, fake dropping it until he smiles. My nose is still throbbing slightly. I dread seeing what it looks like in the mirror, so I fight the mental image of it and focus on Eddie instead.

"You sure you're good?" He runs his hands through his wavy hair. His natural color is a rich brown, close to wet bark. But right now he has leftover summer hair, with kind of auburn and gold bits on top from working outside. Painting shirtless outside. Ahem.

"I'm sure I'm good—it was just a bloody nose. It happens to everyone, even those of us blessed with a specimen such as this." I wave my hands at my nose like it's a game show prize, and Eddie laughs. "You didn't have to miss practice for me." Once the words are out, I blush because it makes his actions sound heroic. "Even though it was just drills."

"I didn't miss it *for* you," he corrects. He gives a wave to someone over my shoulder. Standing at the corner of Maple and Main are a group of his sports buddies, no doubt wondering what could have kept their top forward from showing up. "I missed it *with* you."

He leaves me there, pondering the slight difference, and walks away with a small thumbs-up. "See you tomorrow?"

"Without a doubt," I say and start to walk toward the arched doorway of Any Time Now.

As if it's an afterthought, he adds, "You're a good friend, Cyrie." Then, like it meant nothing, he points to his bloodied sweatshirt. "I'll be up doing laundry all night."

Guys are so confusing. So random. Or at least Eddie is. Before I can comment, he's met up with his friends and been swept away into the group of popular and pretty guys who will probably go to Comet, the trendy diner halfway down Main Street.

Comet is where the Wendy Von Schmedlers and Leslies

and Gossips and fashionistas all hang out. It's where the PBVs drape themselves over the overstuffed red velvet couches and order complicated coffee drinks. It's probably where I'd go, too, if I weren't likely to spend my time there fending off insults or being asked to do people's homework while they make out in the corner.

Instead, I've become a regular at Any Time Now. And the truth is, the place has grown on me.

I walk in and admire the new scene. Any Time Now is run by Hanna Fisher, who graduated from Weston High and had a short-lived but fruitful adventure in Hollywood (she was that pretty-but-quirky redhead on that oceanside teen series). When she came back to town, she opened Any Time Now and decorated it with "borrowed" props from various film sets and television sound stages in LA.

I know all this only because I am such a frequent customer that she tends not to mind if I stay past closing time. She even lets me have free refills on the frozen hot chocolate, the house specialty.

"Look what the lion dragged in," Hanna says from behind the counter, when I walk in.

"I think the expression is, look what the *cat* dragged in." I look around for a table.

"You're way too literal, Cyrie." Hanna folds napkins into neat piles, stacking them so they alternate colors. "Of course that's the expression, but it never made much sense to me. Sure, a cat could drag in a dead mouse or a wounded bird or something, but it couldn't possibly drag in a human. So I substitute lion. Gimme a little space." She smiles at me and adjusts her bonnet.

Normally, the sight of a woman in a bonnet might be surprising, considering I live nowhere near Amish country. But in Any Time Now, I have come to expect anything. Or rather, nothing surprises me in here.

Any Time Now's "thing," as Hanna calls it, is that its décor, food, music, and overall air changes every month. One day a month, usually the last Sunday, she closes the doors, papers shut the windows, and spends hours upon hours with her staff changing the entire restaurant. Last month the whole thing was a Grecian Palace, with the baristas in glamorized togas, white columns adorning the dining area, faux marble painted onto the counter, vines and grape leaves draped from the ceiling, and amazing Greek food served on platters.

Today, I am standing in an amazingly near-perfect replica of a Victorian tea shop. Standing lamps with ornate glass shades cast soft hues of light onto layered rugs. Little round tables, covered by cloths, are topped with three-tiered trays that hold a bounty of finger sandwiches and pastries.

"Celedon? Darjeeling?" Hanna offers.

"Don't call me Darjeeling." I smirk and point to a black raspberry tea on the handwritten menus. "And I'll take a scone while you're at it. Please."

Hanna flits off to deal with other customers and leaves me with a dark blue cloak and bonnet, just in case I want to dress up in theme. Which I don't. Whenever the theme changes, Hanna hangs up extra costumes on the coat rack in hopes people will join in and wear flapper outfits, or kimonos, or—in this case—Victorian garb. I drape the cloak over the handrail, and clear a table so there's enough room for my various books and binders.

I look at the frenzied list we drew up of possible auction items, but before I get sucked into thinking about that, I make myself focus on the task at hand. The task being—college applications and essays.

The applications I'll do mainly online, but the essays take more time. Mr. Reynolds says he has a fail-proof formula for college essays, but he'll only show it to us after we've written a draft of our own.

"Here you are, Miss," trills Hanna in a fake, though totally believable, English accent. "Scones and cream tea."

She sets a currant-dotted scone in front of me and stares a little too long at my face. My hand instantly flies to my nose. "What?"

"Nothing, Miss," says Hanna, still in character.

I look up at her. The ties from her bonnet have come

undone and sway under her chin. If I wore that hat I'd look like a face with a broomstick. She looks adorable, like a hot Holly Hobbie.

I stir a teaspoon of sugar into my teacup and sigh. "Fine. I'll tell you. I got hit in the nose by … someone that I … " I take a pause to consider whether I should admit my feelings for Eddie, and decide against it. No one should know. Once you say that kind of thing out loud, there's no taking it back.

Hanna wipes her hands on her apron. "I'm waiting … "

"It's nothing," I say. "Really."

Hanna shrugs. "Well, you've got that 'nothing' written all over your face."

&

After my tea, and a fruitless hour-plus attempt to write my Columbia University essay—aptly titled "My Greatest Flaw and How It Helps Me"—I clear my teacup, tell Hanna her new theme is great, and get ready to leave. My biggest flaw is clearly my nose, but right now, I can't properly put into words how it's helping me. Maybe because it isn't.

I'm just slinging my bag onto my shoulder when my mom comes in. She's dressed in a bland skirt and jacket, her work outfit, and her cheeks are flushed from walking over from her office.

"I thought I'd find you here," she says, looking around

to take in the change of scenery. She gestures toward Hanna. "She's so talented ... she should have her own television show or something."

"She did, Mom," I say and raise my eyebrows.

"Oh, right." My mother studies my face for a second. She knows better than to ask about the puffiness in the middle of my face. "Ready to go? I figured we could walk home together."

I nod, collect my things, and meet her by the door. We head out together into the fading daylight of our town.

At first glance, Weston seems like your average suburban town settled sometime in the 1700s by Puritans. Whenever we had a field trip to "an important historical site," we would wind up sitting in a circle on the town green looking at the white-steepled church, or the slanting brick building that was once a famous writer's house, or the clapboard structure along Maple Street that a couple hundred years ago housed horses and town meetings, but now is home to a variety of cute clothing and housewares shops.

However, just because our sweet little suburbia looks normal doesn't mean it's average. The truth is, my hometown is a bit peculiar. The library has a pillow pit (during snowstorms you're allowed to sleep there), the PTA controls how we socialize at lunch, and just when you think you've got the place figured out, it changes. Two years ago, for example, after researching the effects of a liberal arts education, the school board switched visual and performing arts from electives to requirements for graduation. And instead of Starbucks and the Gap and all the other chain stores, we have little boutiques and a diner. We have Any Time Now, which is so far from a franchise, you can't even imagine. Weston actually has a town ordinance against such chain stores—not blocking them (because I think that might be illegal), but blocking buildings of a certain height in the downtown area, which basically means that unless someone wanted to open the smallest Best Buy ever, chain stores are a no-go. The retail coffee places from the strip mall fifteen minutes down the road wouldn't survive here—people are loyal to their little cafés. Thus, my beloved Any Time Now.

And Weston's quirky not just because of its lack of well-known eateries. We've got a hermit living in Woodland Hills (the hiking trail area behind the town hall) and we're the proud host of the Street Art Competition (anyone can enter, drawing or painting on the sidewalks and store windows). Also, six years ago, some rich entrepreneur gave the elementary school a few acres of land and now they grow their own food to serve at lunch. And instead of being satisfied with regular school dances and sporting events, the town's obsessed with city-wide themes—carnivals, parties, anything that will draw people out of their Victorian houses and into the community at large.

My mother and I walk the length of the Weston Green, kicking through the first few leaves that have started to fall.

"I can't believe you're a senior!" she says.

"We're not going to have this talk again, are we?" I smile. "I know, I know, you're incredibly sentimental. Your little bird is flying the coop . . . "

"No," she interjects, "I'm just excited to turn your room into a yoga studio when you leave."

My face falls for a nanosecond. "Nice try, Mom." We walk a minute in silence. "Besides, I might not get in anywhere. Then you'll be stuck with me—forever!"

Mom stops and brushes the hair away from my face. "I can think of worse scenarios."

Two little kids go by, one on a bike, one on a scooter. The scooter boy turns to his friend and says—in that overly loud, kid way—"Oh my God! Did you see that thing?"

My mom has witnessed this so many times before with me that she doesn't try to talk over the insult or pretend it didn't happen. She just pats my shoulder. Normally I wouldn't care, either, but far across the green I can see a crowd emptying from Comet. The cheerleaders had stopped by, still in their bright blue and yellow uniforms, and even from this distance I can see Eddie, so tall he towers over the perky pom-pomers.

"I'm so done with this," I say to my mom, and flick my nose.

"Cyrie, don't…" Mom pleads. "Look at yourself—you're incredible. You're funny and smart and the best writer at Weston High."

"But not beautiful…" I say. "Just for once, I'd like that to be in there somewhere among my accolades. I'd even settle for decent-looking."

My mother shakes her head and watches me watch the Comet crowd. "Have you ever considered that maybe 'beautiful' would find its way in there if you'd let it? You're so busy announcing that you're not, that you make it impossible for someone to decide for themselves!"

The fall wind picks up, scattering leaves across the still-green grass, and I pull my sleeves over my hands to keep them warm. "Let's go home." And then, just in case she's forgotten, I add, "Anyway, only four more months and it's gone." I mime snipping my nose, and my mother immediately puts her hand over her mouth.

"Cyrie, please…" she starts. Then she stops. She's probably thinking of her fundraising psychology and how she could get me to reconsider my actions—but if she's come up with a solution, she doesn't vocalize it. Instead, she buttons her tweed blazer and nudges me to keep walking, past the shops, the antiques, and the rest of our quaint little town toward home.

I tell her about the auction. I know I'm excited, because I

start talking really fast, telling her all about the *Word's* plans. I even tell her I'm working with Eddie.

"You two seem to be paired together a lot," she says, trying to get out her house keys. She has an annoying habit of taking them out when we're still three blocks away. She also turns her turn signal on way early in the car, so I guess it's the same thing—always being overly prepared.

"Yeah, I guess so," I say, as if I've only now just noticed that Eddie is in nearly all my classes and partnered with me most of the time. "At least he does the work. Leyla Christianson is stuck with Billy Riggs in her History hands-on, and all he did was to offer to pay for the poster-making supplies."

"How is Leyla these days?" Mom asks as she jingles the keys.

"Good," I say, picturing Leyla and her contagious laugh, her friendly (if too perfect) face. "She's actually a lot more . . . she's a better friend than I ever thought she'd be."

"I'm glad." My mother sets her bag down on the front porch, and fiddles with her enormous key ring until she finds the brass one that unlocks our front door. Like many of the houses in Weston, ours is historic—and the front door still has one of those buck-toothed keys that you have to fit in just right or the door won't budge.

I think about calling Leyla to do homework tonight, about the college essay that plagues me, and about how I'll try not to look at last year's yearbook picture of Eddie. (He's caught in action on the soccer field during a practice, with no shirt. Bless that heat wave!)

Mom opens the door with a small kick and goes inside. I stay outside for a minute, enjoying the early fall evening. It's easy, in quiet moments like this, to think about being with Eddie—on the porch doing newspaper stuff, or joking around playing with a football in the grass like we're part of an Abercrombie spread, or holding hands while we sit in comfortable silence. I take a seat on the white wicker bench on the porch and imagine him next to me. A smile creeps across my face. Then the sun starts to set, casting its glow across the porch and creating shadows that make everything look longer and bigger than it already is.

five

"You so have to come, it's gonna be great!" Leyla says into the phone the next night. I can hear her music in the background. She starts humming along with "Are You Leading Me On" and says, "I love General Public. I'm putting this song on my fundraising mix."

At school today, I came up with the idea of getting random students to burn CDs of their favorite songs for an auction grab bag. Leyla mentioned the idea at the *Word* meeting, and everyone loved it. Of course, I was glad to have the mix grab bag approved, and the fact that Leyla got credit for it ... well, at first I felt weird-slash-annoyed, but then my intellectual side took over and I figured that as long as the money gets raised, it's no big deal. Plus, it's not like Leyla meant to pilfer my brainstorm. She said it just slipped out—and to call her on it would be petty and useless.

"There's no way I'm going," I say, then brush my teeth while I wait for her response. She knows she's got to come up with a damn good argument to sway me into spending my Friday night at the school gym. "I spend enough of my waking hours trapped in that low-ceilinged, fluorescent-lighted cave. I don't need to trek back there voluntarily."

Granted, the school gym won't look like the sweat-infused basketball haven it normally is; rather, it will be a jousting hall for the Weston High's Night of Knights, in which maidens and masters of the sword alike get to dress up and drink grape juice out of gray plastic goblets that are supposed to make everything feel authentic. The drama crowd has been busy preparing since August, making sets, painting scenes, and sewing flags. Not really my kind of fun but, then again, maybe the whole town's just trying to rally against the puritanical roots set down by Pilgrims way back when.

"Okay—here are my top three reasons why you should go," Leyla says. "I'm even turning my music off so you can hear me better."

"This sounds important," I say, rinsing. "I'll even hold off on flossing until you're done." I leave the bathroom and go to my room. Our house is actually two buildings put together—a tiny farm cottage from the 1800s, which is the main house, and a silo my parents connected to the house and converted into a sort-of tower. If I were a princess-type girl, I would have endless fodder for daydreaming. My room occupies the whole top part, so I live in a perfectly round bedroom. It's slightly bizarre, but it works.

I'm on the floor, staring out the window at the full fall moon as Leyla talks. "Okay, the first reason to go is that you're a senior. Since you let your social life pass you by in other years, this is your last chance to see the Knights joust. You wouldn't want to get to graduation and regret not being an active part of the class, right?"

"Maybe. Next reason?" I prop myself up on a pile of cushions and will myself not to reach for last year's yearbook, in which a frozen-in-time Eddie Roxanninoff waits smiling and shirtless. On my desk, also frozen in time, is my still-blank college essay: "My Greatest Flaw and How It Helps Me." I'm beginning to think I need a new topic.

"Next reason: everyone makes asses out of themselves, and you always appreciate that."

"That, Leyla, is true. I do enjoy laughing both at myself and at others." Last year, I happened by the spring Rose Gala (held outside the school near the track) and for a second thought about joining in, despite the fact that I was wearing sweatpants and a tank top and everyone else was clad in dresses and suits. Just when I thought about nosing in—verb intentionally used—I was confronted by Darla Dinkins. One thing led to another, and after a drunk Darla asked if I could "smell the roses all the way from town," I let loose on her grades, which reek. Truth be told, I could've let her go with just that—she was sloppy and tipsy—but once I got going I didn't stop. I told her how everyone saw her—just a face in the crowd who will be voted Least Likely To Be Remembered. Then I left.

"There's no other reason, is there?" I ask, thinking back to that night, how I walked back alone to a dark house. Why do that again?

"And..." Leyla lets out a big breath, which she does when she's thinking hard. When she first joined the *Word*, I actually used to count how many long breaths it took her to get through one article pitch—her record was fourteen. She's much better now, but still lapses now and again. "Point two and a half, which—fine, you'll probably tell me it makes four points, but anyway—"

"Leyla, it's getting late. You'll have to persuade me with this last thing. I'd so much rather kick back with a movie and pizza on Friday than watch Josh and the jocks poke each other with sharp sticks. Wait—on second thought, that sounds okay..."

"Cyrie... don't make me go alone." Her voice is small and quiet.

"You'll hardly be alone. You have Wendy Von Schmedler, Jill, Leslie, all those guys. You know, your *other friends*..."

Leyla's voice gets softer. "You're my friend."

Outside, the moon illuminates my street and makes it seem bigger than it really is, at least from up here. "I know, I know—I didn't mean it like that. It's just … "

"No, you don't have to explain. I get it. But I'm not really *with* Wendy and those guys when I'm with them, if you get what I mean. It's not … real." She coughs and takes a breath.

"I just have visions of standing there by myself while Wendy and Jill lure you back to the dark side."

"No. No. It won't be like that." Leyla gets back to her point, her voice higher with excitement. "But listen, you always say we need supporting facts for our stories, right? And for op-ed pieces? Well, you like plays and studying literature from other eras … and Any Time Now is your favorite place, so you could imply from that—"

"Infer. You infer *from* something." I fiddle with my curtains; they're made of sheer navy silk and appliquéd with stars. On the floor are oversized cushions, some square, some circular, in contrasting fabrics. I made most of them last year during a fit of pre-exam jitters and vacation boredom-slash-inspiration after watching one too many home décor shows. I pick up a silvery bolster cushion and tuck it behind my neck as I lean against one of the curved walls. The biggest problem with a room shaped like mine is that there's no real place to lean comfortably; I would normally cozy up in a corner, but that is mathematically impossible.

"Whatever. Couldn't you *infer*, from that, that you are a person who kind of likes dressing up, or the idea of romance?"

I blush as soon as she says "romance." Not so much because the word is inherently embarrassing but because I immediately connect romance with Eddie, and that whole thing is definitely blushworthy. I'm just not the crush kind of person—at least, I haven't been. "Sure. Romance would be nice."

"So, that's one point for going."

"Night of Knights is hardly romantic—I mean, you've got the pom-pom squad gowned like Maid Marian, the theater crew doing their Shakespearean over-the-top drama. When you combine that with the potential for indirect injury…" I trail off, distracted by the memory of Eddie bashing my *magnus nasus* and the picture in front of me (having given into my yearbook-drooling urge). I stare at two-dimensional Eddie, in lust and love.

"Can I just tell you my last reason?" Leyla asks. Her dad yells in the background for her to get off the phone. "I gotta go."

"Wait—just give it up—what's the last push, your final selling point for what is sure to be a thrilling evening of high school high jinks?"

"I've got a big-time secret. If you come with me to Knights, I'll tell you!" Leyla is a master of this kind of thing, garnered from her days cheerleading with the Gossips and their queen, Wendy.

"If you think I'm going to fall for some lame … "

"You know you're a sucker for a scoop—think of this as the big headline for fall." Then Leyla screams, "Just a second!"

"I take it that was meant for your dad … listen, I'll think about it, okay? But I'm not making any promises." We hang up without a formal goodbye. I tuck my legs up to my chest and close the yearbook. Even without Eddie in front of me, I can still see him. And I can still see my retro red clock, which tells me it's late and time for bed.

In the morning, my dad brings me breakfast on a tray and leaves it outside my room. He knocks twice to let me know the food's there. It's not that he treats me like his little princess or anything, it's that he owes me breakfast delivered to my door for the entire semester. This past summer, he made the colossal mistake of betting me about meaningless musical trivia. Dorky though my recall for artists, release dates, and cover versions may be, it's still a strength, and even Dad knew it was a slight risk.

We were out at the Beach Shack (which is, oddly, a lakeside restaurant), and over the outside speakers came "Always Something There to Remind Me."

"I love this song!" I said.

"This is way before your time," Dad said. Mom nodded as she munched the salsa and chips. "I was in grad school when this came out."

"You mean, when this cover version came out."

"This is a cover?" Mom asked. Despite liking music, she has no interest in who sings what or the name of songs or even getting the lyrics right.

"This is Naked Eyes," I said, pressing my point.

"Right. The original artist," Dad said. "I remember because it was all New Wave and one of the teaching assistants thought it was drivel and I agreed."

"Well, you don't have to like it, but you have to admit it's a cover. Burt Bacharach wrote the original." I locked eyes with him. "Not a cover." My voice gets steely when I'm sure of something, when I'm about to engage in verbal combat.

Dad shook his head and reached for a chip, and then the waitress brought my root beer in the bottle. Trying to be casual, I put the bottle to my mouth. But because my nose sticks so far out, it's really hard to drink like that. I usually ask for a straw or look around for a wide-mouthed cup, but I'd forgotten. Maybe Dad felt bad for me, or maybe he really didn't know as much musical trivia as me, but he flagged down the waitress, got a straw, and handed it to me. Then he said, "I bet you're wrong."

"I'll bet you," I said. I didn't mention I'd just, coincidentally, put the original song on a summer mix for Leyla. "But don't bet big, Dad, because you'll surely lose." I tried not to insult him—or at least I didn't want to, but the words slipped out. "I mean, you may be a lot of things, but a musical maven isn't one of them. You're too old to play this game." Once that last sentence came out, prickles of regret started piercing by neck. "I mean…"

"I admire your confidence, Cyrie," Dad said, at least feigning immunity to my words. He rolled his shirtsleeves up. "But you're in for a solid month of dishes."

"Raise the stakes—live big, Dad." The regret eased as he challenged me. My voice went right back to combat zone. "How about a whole fall of dishes?"

Mom clapped her hands. "Oh—that sounds good. Do that, Dan."

My father nodded. "And on the slim chance I'm incorrect? What do I have to do?"

I thought about it. I thought about what wouldn't be so bad that I'd feel guilty, and what would make my senior fall feel special. "Breakfast at Any Time Now, every day," I said, knowing he'd never go for it.

"I'm not spending your future college tuition on muffins," Dad said. "How about breakfast brought right to your door—it'll give you extra time to sleep or primp or whatever you do in the mornings."

"Sounds like a plan."

We finished our dinner, and I went home to show him just how correct I was. And since the Tuesday after Labor Day, it's been a steady tray of eggs, waffles, bagels, cereal and bananas, and even my favorite, chocolate chip pancakes. I suspect that the novelty will wear off soon and by mid-fall he'll drop a box of Rice Krispies outside my door, but I'm enjoying my winnings so far.

Today my breakfast bounty (or cornucopia) is a bowl of fruit salad with yogurt and granola. Go health!

I spoon in a mouthful and read my emails.

> *Hey Chief,*
>
> *Just checking in to make sure you're really really okay after my klutzy move the other day. I think my sweatshirt's permanently stained, but I think it gives the article of clothing character—like I play rugby or something. Anyway, I have a bunch of leads for the auction, so we should probably set up a time to meet. Are you free tonight?*
>
> *Rox*

Even though he signs it Rox, I respond with:

> *Eddie—*

From a legal standpoint, you're safe. My lawyer told me I could sue you for damages, but I won't—I'm just that nice.

Glad to hear my injury and loss of blood has given your Weston sweatshirt its much-needed character and charm. Always glad to help.

Tonight's fine—I'll be working on my essays (and that lab assignment) at home after dinner, so you can come by then.

Cyrie

I press send before I can reread it too many times, checking for signs of giving away my feelings. I think it was safe enough, and hope that telling him to come over doesn't sound too much like asking for a date. Then I remember that he was the one suggesting we get together, so I won't worry.

It's little things, like these emails, that make me want to tell Leyla about my old-fashioned crush on Eddie, just so I can talk to someone and get another perspective. I could tell Hanna at Any Time Now (she's fairly removed from possible secret-spillage) or even my dad, but part of me feels like if I tell someone, all they'll say is what I already know—that it's just wishful thinking, and nothing more.

The first part of the day passes without much of note—except that when I have downtime in the corridors, when I'm swapping one text for another at my locker, my mind drifts to what, if anything, Leyla might be keeping from me. What could her "big secret" be, aside from making the honor roll, which (though I support her in her quest for higher brainage) I don't think she's pulled off quite yet. Then again, it could be something more scandalous—like the rumors her old flame Josh spread. (According to him, when Leyla was a cheerleader she was lot more interested in seeing him take off his sports uniforms than in watching the games.)

The morning comes and goes, and then it's post-lunch, that time when a sleepy haze wafts over all of us. To make the lethargy worse, I have study hall.

Sitting next to Sarah Jensen is the only time I feel totally outpaced while studying—especially in study hall, a place that defies its name since most people feel free to do nothing. While many of them choose to pass notes, whisper, or even nod off, Sarah is efficiently completing all her homework and—from the looks of it—all her college essays.

"Early decision—Harvard," she says to me without my even asking. We have an unspoken respect, based primarily on our GPAs and, I suspect, a little on our lack of social status. But while she is cloistered off—an academic ace but a complete loner, in Latin club and so on—I'm different. It's like I'm in the social scene, but just on the outskirts—close enough to know exactly what's going on, but aware that the people, parties, and hook-ups are still an arm's length (or other body part) away. "What about you?"

"Huh?" I look at Sarah's even hair-part and her careful printing, and I can't imagine what she's writing in her Harvard application unless it's something like *Why I'm Perfect* or *It's difficult being the top-ranked student at my school.*

But, of course, I know too well that those titles leave out a certain aspect of life—like having one. My freshman and sophomore years, I swear all I did was study. I earned straight A's and extra credit on top of those grades, thought about going out for track (I'm a decent long distance runner) but wound up choosing tennis, joined the Italian club (after Latin, romance languages come easily), and even tried my hand at studio art (I suck), and could technically list eighteen extracurriculars on my pre-college list. I was so busy I didn't really notice my lack of friends, my utter lack of romantic potential, and the general void where a life beyond school-work would normally be.

It wasn't until the end of sophomore year when, from my place in the bleachers at graduation, I realized I didn't know even a fifth of the seniors. I'd never see these people again, even the ones who made fun of me in the lunchroom, and yet I felt like I missed them. I missed knowing names and faces and kidding around with people (kidding takes time, and I never had time between classes and courses and credits). Watching the other sophomores in their best-friend pairs, I had to admit I was jealous. The first step to getting a friend and a life, I figured, was scaling down my crazy activity roster.

Cutting back was easy, actually. The *Word* was by far the place I felt happiest. The stories came fluidly, I enjoyed the research, and the staff (even the jocky kids who spelled "you are" as "your" rather than "you're," or the semi-mean girls who were nice to me when they needed help with a lead sentence, then trashed my nose or sweater later) were all okay. I let my clubs and committees slide; this year, I even let tennis go. But I always kept the *Word*, determined to become editor.

I announced to my parents that I was drastically reducing my level of frantic.

"We're so proud of you," Mom said, trying to flap her arms and breathe in a pattern that was supposed to help her abdominal muscles. "Damn these things," she added, and stopped the DVD she was mimicking. "I'm going back to old-fashioned running."

"Careful of your knees," Dad said to her. Then he stared at my face in careful consideration. "This is monumental, Cyrie."

"Oh yeah?" I tapped my foot—I was glad to have a good relationship with my parents, but I couldn't stand being a part of their weird Sunday afternoon yoga/newspapers/carrot juice recap of the week, not to mention their odd tendencies toward cardio workouts and rearranging the furniture.

"Yes," Dad said. "It's a big deal when you realize your limitations."

"You have it totally wrong there, Dad. This isn't about me not being able to keep up with all this. It's just that..." Outside the house, a carload of Weston students (Westies, as they are sometimes known) honked, music blaring. "I'm ready for more, actually. Just not clubs and classes." Mom stood up and stretched. "I'm going to get a social life."

"I stand corrected," Dad (ever the lawyer) said, feeling his weekend beard. "But it's still a big step for you, Cyr. And I think I speak for the both of us when I say we're happy for you, and..." (he looked at my mom) "...it's about time!"

So when Sarah Jensen asks me where I'm applying for early decision, I can answer her without feeling bad about my strategy. Once I'd realized I was using extracurriculars and my straight A's as a cover (a cover not just for my nose, but for my general shyness in the social arena), I felt even more solid about freeing myself. It's not like I went from nothing to Prom Queen, but I now know people's names. I've become part of the social fabric at Weston. And since meeting Leyla, I kind of have a best friend—or whatever the word is for a best friend who is technically in a totally different social group than you.

"I'm not applying early," I tell Sarah Jensen. She looks like I've just announced I'm a slug trapped in human form.

"Why not?" She allows her pencil to stop moving across the page, and sets her pointer finger on her open textbook to mark her place while she recovers from my shocking news.

"You know, I'm just not sure I could commit completely to one school. What if there's another one I'd rather go to? I mean, it's not a sure thing no matter what I do, but I'd like to feel like I have choices. Come April, I just want to feel like *I* made a decision, too, you know?"

"But you've been planning on Columbia, talking about it forever," Sarah says. Something in her mouth makes her look sad, like I've hit on something maybe she's thought about, too.

"I know, I know. And I would probably love it there. And maybe I'll get in—and maybe I won't." I look around at all the people studying, the seniors who will all be dispersed across the country at college, or taking a year off, or in Eddie's case maybe going to Oxford. It's hard to think beyond high school when you're in it, but I try to explain my point of view to Sarah. "Making choices is part of what makes us different from animals, right? We not only know how to feed ourselves, but we decide what to eat and when and how much. What's something you like?"

"To eat?" Sarah wrinkles her forehead.

"Yeah, like mac and cheese, or egg salad … "

"I hate anything egg-related," she informs me.

"I'll remember that in case we ever have brunch, okay? But my point is—you love candy necklaces." I point to the one currently around her neck. Since eighth grade she's been crunching away on her special sweet treat at least once a week. Just the smell of those necklaces makes me feel academic pressure.

Sarah's hand flies to her neck and she touches her beloved candy couture. "I do."

"But do you love them because you really really love them, or are you just used to eating them?"

Sarah thinks a minute. "So, because you always planned on Columbia University as your goal, your quest, you're now doubting the validity of that desire?"

In the doorway, I spot a familiar shade of green that can only mean one thing: Eddie Roxanninoff and his incredibly well-faded Dartmouth T-shirt—a hand-me-down from his older brother, who graduated Weston three years ago. I love seeing Eddie in this shirt because it reflects who he is. It's comfy, soft (I felt it once when I smushed a mosquito on his back; he was grateful), brings out the moss hue in his eyes, and—most importantly—is that article of clothing that will one day be loaned to a girlfriend and never given back. Many a night I have piled my floor cushions up and wondered if I could ever be the one who'd get that T-shirt.

"Sarah, look, all I mean is that—for me—I realized that I want a choice. I want to imagine who I could be at Columbia or Amherst or Stanford or Harvard..." I watch Sarah make a mental note that I'll be competing for what she sees as her spot at Harvard. "Best-case scenario is that I get into two places and pick what feels right at the time."

Sarah nods, still a little sad, and immediately goes back to taking notes for her essay. I watch her nibble from the candy necklace and then, before I talk more with her, before I scribble my own notes (Columbia or elsewhere, I have got to get going on those essays), before I even have time to try not to stare at Eddie, he's in front of me. Even though his soccer buddies and his best friend, Louie Goldman, are all on the other side of the room, Eddie comes over to me first.

"Hey," he says and crouches down next to me, whispering so Mrs. Talbot doesn't tap him on the shoulder and tell him to leave. "How's it going?"

"Good. I'm in the process of not writing my application essays." I point to the blank paper in front of me and am really glad I never doodle Eddie's initials. As I watch his face and catch myself grinning just because he's near me, I decide that "crush" is a bad word. Or, it's not apt. In the love thesaurus, crush is not the best description of my feelings. More like "inflammation," if that didn't conjure up athlete's foot. Or "passion," if that didn't call to mind soap operas. Maybe "granulate"—I feel like dissolving into a million pieces near him, and at the same time there's an ease to our conversations that I haven't found with anyone else ... ever.

"I'm sure you'll have a unique and stunningly written essay," Eddie says without the slightest trace of irony—he actually believes this. He gives a head nod to Louie, who coughs "Rox" under his breath. Then Eddie leans even closer to me and says, "Want to walk to Drama together later?"

All aspiring graduates at Weston High must take Harold Connaught's theatrical components class, given that Drama is a now a senior requirement. The academic committee feels that the improvs and random one-acts we have to perform will help us prepare for college interviews, job interviews, and life as we know it. It's not bad, though; Harold's the only teacher we get to call by his first name.

"Sure," I say, still smiling, and aware that the angle Eddie's crouching at does nothing to help minimize my schnoz. I try not to cover it—not only because I can't, but because it would just draw more attention to it. "But you're not in my drama class."

Eddie stands up, about to go over to Louie (who has *The Mayor of Casterbridge* on his head like it's a hat). Jennie Karn and Minnie Lester, twin hotties (who aren't so much biological twins as attractive seniors who dress, sound, and act disturbingly alike), are trying not to giggle as they fawn over him.

"Correction. Up until *today* I wasn't in your drama class."

Eddie sweeps his hand through his hair and scratches his cheek.

"Why'd you switch?" I ask. Eddie blushes. Or maybe it's just the sunlight coming in the big windows. No … definitely a blush.

He shrugs. "Let's just say it fits my schedule better."

I raise my eyebrows. "Your schedule?" With our ever-shifting block A and block B schedules, no one really knows what meets when. But hey, this feels like flirting. As soon as I think this, my heart starts to pound. Maybe Leyla won't be the only one with a secret at Night of Knights. If I go, maybe I'll have a little uncommon knowledge that I can choose to share with her. Or not.

"Schedule … or something."

Eddie gives some guy-sign to Louie that I don't understand and then says, "See you in a few."

I watch him walk off, and I have just the tiniest bit of hope that I might be that "something."

six

The Weston High snack bar is run by parents, and a portion of the profits go to the Weston High scholarship fund. So I feel compelled, not just by hunger but by good will, to purchase a pack of Mini Oreos. These nickel-sized cookies are highly underrated in the world of snack foods. Sure, the big ones are good, great with cold milk and the subject of a song that's just way too easy to get stuck in your head. But the little cookies are perfect: sweet and crunchy, and the individual packets are small enough that you don't feel grotesque afterwards.

I drop my money onto the snack bar and Mrs. Von

Schmedler, Wendy's mother and today's cashier, gives me a look of complete and utter pity—just like her daughter's gaze.

"Thank you," I say and collect my change.

Mrs. Von Schmedler is one of those mothers who tries everything to defy her age. She works out incessantly, dresses in fashions meant for *Teen Vogue*, and uses words and phrases she picks up from Wendy, all while looking eerily statue-like and every bit her age. I doubt she knows how cruel her daughter can be, but I'm sure she's aware of Wendy's queen-like social position. Probably, if you delved into Wendy's psyche, you'd find a lot of pressure from her mom and learn how picked-upon Wendy herself feels—which in turn could be the cause of Wendy's gossipy, mean habits. I think this as I watch Mrs. Von Schmedler stare at me, and wonder if I should switch my future major from journalism to psychology.

"I hear great things about your upcoming auction. You're such an involved student, Cyrie." Mrs. Von Schmedler gives me her widest bleached smile. She sounds so nice, so complimenting, that I want to believe her—but I know better.

"Well, it's not really *my* auction, but it's great to help organize it." Then I gesture to the snack bar like it's a game show prize, and draw on another of my mother's fundraising tactics: sweeten each sentence just enough to boost the ego of the person, but not enough so they call you on it. "You do wonderful fundraising things yourself…"

I hope that the compliment will distract her from the

path she's going down, which will inevitably contort the meaning of "involved" to "loserly." She'll probably mention a party I didn't go to or some big event Wendy has planned, in which I am not included.

"I do try to do my part," Mrs. V says, checking her hair in the reflection of the glass refrigerator door. In the years I've known Wendy, her mother's hair has gone from that shade of brown that's just before black, to lighter brown, to ashy brown, to its current state of blonde. She's actually a really pretty woman, but her frown lines give away her inner murkiness. "Charity is so important, don't you think?"

What *do* I think? Mom lesson #3—don't ever miss a moment. So I say, "Longfellow once said, 'the life of a man consists not in seeing visions and in dreaming dreams, but in active charity and in willing service.'"

I watch Mrs. V nod, her brow furrowed, until she remembers that this is likely to cause wrinkles. She pats her fingers on her suspiciously unwrinkled face. I've positioned myself rather well, considering she was out to attack me at first—or at least that's how I felt. Now I'm able to reach for what I want. "And speaking of charity … how would you feel about donating something really fantastic for the auction?"

Mrs. Von Schmedler hands someone a cheese stick, counts their change, and turns back to me. "Maybe … "

I snap to attention. "You'll get full credit on the programs, of course." It's easy to appeal to her vanity.

"I might be able to swing something—just how big were you thinking?" She narrows her gaze, not wanting to be played.

Now comes the tricky part: trying, but not too hard. If I'm too needy, she'll do her speed-walk away. "Ideally? A two-week free rental at your lakeside cabin," I say.

The Von Schmedlers' cabin is the stuff of legend. When Wendy's older sister Gretchen was a senior, she threw parties that were rumored to have made Sunday Styles headlines in the *New York Times*. The cabin itself has been photographed for *Architectural Digest* and *InStyle*, and the lake and land have been used in countless movies. The pictures are so beautiful, and the location so ideal, I've always wanted to go there. Not that I'd be able to afford the rental (and even if I did, I don't know who I'd bring). But if it were in the auction, at least someone like me would benefit from the place.

"Not a chance," Mrs. V says in response, and makes a face like she's just tasted whole milk in her non-fat cappuccino. Then she studies my face, which I have carefully frozen in expectation. Mom says that if you let people see your disappointment right away, they are less inclined to give anything since they feel that there's no way to please you. If you stay frozen, they will give you a counter-offer, which is what you wanted all along.

This is, of course, if you don't speak. Whoever speaks first loses. Which is all fine; I'm not one who needs to ramble, needs to check in and break an uncomfortable silence. If I'm feared for my verbal eviscerations, then my silence is all the more effective because no one expects it.

Mrs. Von Schmedler stares at me, unblinking. I stare back. The call bell rings. We have a paper meeting scheduled for after lunch today, then comes the drama class I've been waiting for. Or rather, the walk to drama class that I've been longing for.

Even though the rush of students heading to class has come and gone, I don't budge. Finally, as the second, shorter, bell rings, Mrs. Von Schmedler breaks. "I meant it about the two weeks—that's just not going to happen. What I will do is this." She gets her purse and writes something down on a personalized notecard. "Run along now, Cyrie. And good luck with your event."

Play it right, and ye shall receive.

I wait until I'm inside the *Word* office to look at what she's written.

"We got our first big item," I announce to everyone who happens to be near (in this case, Mr. Reynolds, Linus, Jocky Josh, and Leslie—Eddie has a half hour of personal rowing training today). "The Von Schmedler's cabin for all of New Year's weekend!"

"Nice!" Josh pats my back. "That'll go for a lot."

"Awesome—I'm so bidding on that," Leslie says to one of her fashion-maven friends. The whole clique will probably chip in together and bid on the place, and all they'll do is make revolting drink concoctions. But hey, at least it's for a good cause.

Linus, dressed in a blue oxford button-down and cords, takes off his glasses and comes over to me. He signs *well done* and then adds, "That's such a good snag on the cabin."

"Thanks. Oh—you have a little lettuce on your shirt." I pluck a piece of salad off.

Linus watches me remove the vegetable fragment and bites his lip like he does when he's getting ready to pitch a story to me and Mr. Reynolds. "Can I talk to you about something?" he asks.

"Sure. But if you're trying to get out of that article on standardized testing, you can forget it." I check the story board while Linus taps his pen into his palm. "We've already factored in the space, and Leyla did the layout." Leyla, while still not comfortable writing anything, turns out to have great spatial ability—she can do the layout of the whole paper in her head.

"No, I'm down with the story. This isn't…" he trails off, adjusts his glasses, looks over his shoulder, and coughs. "Um, you know how you always say not to bury your lead?"

Burying the lead is the kiss of death in good journalism.

If you don't start off strong, you've lost your reader before they even know what's at stake. "Yeah, I do say that," I nod.

"Well, I want a good lead, so to speak. So I want your advice."

I turn to him. His face looks serious—not his usual sarcastic glances and shy smiles. "I'm guessing this is not paper-related," I say.

"Correct," says Linus. "Are you free later?"

I check my watch for no good reason except that whenever someone asks me what I'm doing later—this minute, today, next year—I feel compelled to check my watch. "I'm actually not," I tell him, remembering I have a double dose of Eddie—first en route to drama, and then potentially at my house tonight for, um, auction stuff. "But we could go to Any Time Now right after class tomorrow?"

Linus shakes his head. "I'm covering Night of Knights, remember?" Night of Knights—while the event holds zero appeal for me, Leyla is going and maybe she has a point: I'm a senior, and I should go to things this year just so I don't regret it. And aren't you supposed to regret the things you haven't done more than the things you actually do?

I open my mouth to say of course I remember that Linus is writing the Night of Knights feature. He's one of the only writers we have who can reliably handle the pressure of writing, editing, and proofing an article by Monday publication.

Plus, I assigned the piece. "Linus, I..." But I'm interrupted by Eddie.

He appears at the doorway, his hair wet from showering. He waves to me, and I notice his cheeks are flushed. I tell myself the blush is from his workout, but maybe a tiny bit is due to seeing me? It's a slim chance—but not as impossible as I used to think.

"I want to help you, Linus, I do... maybe IM me later?"

Linus shakes his head. "I'm not into the screen thing. Let's just try to hang out at some point this weekend."

I nod, and give Eddie a "one minute" sign so I can duck to the bathroom before Drama. Without knowing more about Linus' situation, it's hard to predict how I'll help him. Most likely, he wants to petition Reynolds for a better title (staff writer isn't the catchiest of terms for college applications). But it could be something more hidden—he could like someone, and want to ask them out. But in that case, I'm not exactly the go-to girl. He'd be better off asking someone else for advice. Unless—I think back to our canoe ride this summer. He met me at my house, packed a picnic, paid for the boat even though I insisted on splitting the cost, and listened to everything I said. When I think about it like that, it feels like we went on a date...

What if Linus—my buddy, my paper pal—likes me? There's no doubt that he's adorable and smart and all that, but up until this moment in the girls' bathroom, with its ugly green-hued lighting and cracked tiles, I've never thought about Linus with even a remote romantic interest. But ... if there were a guy who could overlook my nose, my giant feature, the unfortunate center of my face, Linus would be that guy. He's the advertisement for "beauty comes from within." He's serious and sensitive and always a little disheveled (like with the lettuce on his shirt, or on the days he's buttoned his shirt wrong or his socks don't match). And he just doesn't care.

Before I can complete my thoughts on this matter, it's time to go. I do one last check in the mirror—jeans, fitted V-neck shirt, boots, clean hair—and push open the squeaky door. Just like I hoped, Eddie is leaning against the wall opposite the door, waiting just for me.

Weston High is U-shaped, and Drama is held in the small old auditorium at one end of the U. So Eddie and I have the entire length of the school to walk together. The marathon journey produces a whole bunch of looks, a couple of giggles, and one shout-out: "Hey Rox, where'd you get the hood ornament?"

Eddie pretends not to hear this—or maybe he really doesn't, he's so wrapped up in his thoughts.

"Care to share?" I ask and elbow him in the ribs.

Care to Share was last year's school motto, and Eddie

smiles at my use of it. He turns to me and strikes a soap opera stance, clutching my shoulders. "Cyrie, I will always care to share with you." Then he looks at an invisible camera and says, "Stay tuned for It's Your Turn to Learn! And other school phrases next … "

He releases his hands from my shoulders. I can still feel the warmth from where he touched me, but I keep moving, past the science center, past the lockers and classrooms and students staring at us. It's as though the thought of us together is scandalous.

"Seriously," I say, trying again. "What's up?"

We're at the doorway to Drama when Eddie lowers his voice and finally tells me. "I've been meaning to talk to you about something. It's kind of important." He blushes, again, and looks away from me. "It's kind of weird to say it out loud … but … I like someone."

I don't know what to say. The cold linoleum school tiles spin as I feel my pulse take off. "I see," I respond, even though I don't see at all.

"This person … this girl … she's … " Eddie pulls me over to the corner of the classroom and whispers, "She's different, right?"

He looks at me, waiting for my confirmation. Then, suddenly, I get it. Right in the doorway to drama class, in the middle of high school, in the middle of Weston, the whole world stops on its axis—he likes me. Eddie Roxanninoff likes me.

"She *is* different," I say. "But..."

And before we can go any further, Harold Connaught claps his hands and signals that class is starting. "To be continued?" Eddie gives me a special look. A deep look. And a quick hug.

"Sure—to be continued," I say into his chest. I try to regain control of my body as I take a seat in the semi-circle of chairs arranged near the small stage.

Harold stands with his hands clasped behind his back. His corduroy pants are dark brown, his shirt white, and his ever-popular bow tie red-and-yellow striped. He looks like he should be on the cover of a clothing catalogue, but instead has chosen to grace us with his presence in Senior Dramatics.

"What's under the sheet?" asks Kristin Murphy, pointing to a covered item on a table in the center of the circle.

"That is the subject of today's class," explains Harold. I'm sitting next to Eddie and trying to pay attention while my brain retraces the conversation we just had—could he like me? As of this morning I'd have said the odds weren't good, but after the walk to class—and the blushing—and the touching—I'd say it just might be possible.

"Cyrie, you go first," Harold says and gestures at me to get up, which I do even though I now have no idea what the drama exercise is about. "Go on."

Eddie gets up and says, "I'll go, too." He gives me a quick

wink, to let me know he saw me spacing out and is coming to my figurative rescue.

"Fine."

Harold Connaught whips the sheet off of the mystery item and reveals ... a box resembling an oversized shoe box. "Now—this is where the senses come into play. Step up to the box, place both hands inside, and feel."

A collective groan from two-thirds of the class. I have no idea, as I approach the dreaded darkness of the box, how much will change when I put my hands inside. But before I do anything, Harold continues.

"Sensory experiences are like memories—you don't know which ones are important until after the fact. But in acting you've got to convince your audience that you're going through something—experiencing it—for the first time." He waves his arms around, rolling his hands as though singing "The Wheels on the Bus." "Again and again, for the first time."

He motions for Eddie and me to put our hands in the box—which we do, though I can't help but mumble, "There better not be eyeballs in here." Halloween isn't far away, and this is reminding me of those haunted houses where you plunge your hand into a bowl of "eyeballs" that turn out to be peeled grapes.

From the rest of the class I hear a few giggles and one low, but discernible, "better than a bunch of noses." I look up, about to feel the balloon of happiness inside me pop. In an instant, all the good feelings from finding out that Eddie likes me could evaporate. And why? Just because some idiot makes one little comment? I breathe deeply and say nothing. It's not decency that keeps me quiet, but Eddie's eyes locked on mine.

"As you move your hands around inside," Harold informs everyone, "you'll come across objects that might feel familiar. But are they?" He holds up a key. "Is a key felt with the hands the same key we see with our eyes?" Eddie and I fight the urge to laugh. Harold Connaught's fun, but he tends toward the overly dramatic.

I slide my left hand over soft fabric. Velvet, I think, and my fingers find a circular object. A button? No, a—

"I think I've got a shoelace," Eddie says. He's far enough away from my hands that I can't feel the lace to check whether he's correct.

Harold nods. "Cyrie—you find something, too."

I search for something recognizable. "A giant paper clip?"

"Perfect for clipping your ... " A giggle starts from the audience but is silenced by Harold's teacherly gaze. "Yes, a paper clip." Just as he says this, my hands find something else: Eddie's hands. Without changing his facial expression in the slightest, he gives my hands a squeeze. I fight the urge to shriek or climb over the box and grab him.

"And now we'll add more hands to mix," Harold says, waving someone over from the doorway.

Leyla emerges with her eyes cast downward, her hair in front of her face, and a sweatshirt around her waist. She glances at me before she sticks her hands into the box, and I give her my *I have a secret now, too* look. She makes her eyes wide and coughs to let me know she understands. It's great to finally have a friendship where we can communicate without words. Which, I realize, may also be the point of this bizarre box exercise: to experience something without relying on your preconceived notions of what it is.

"I feel a toothbrush," Leyla says, her brow furrowed as though she's really concentrating on the task at hand.

"Me, too," Eddie says. Ever-competitive, he is probably snaking his way around the box to find every item on offer. My own hands flail, bumping into a sponge, a pacifier, something unidentifiable, a sock I hope isn't dirty, and then, finally, the toothbrush.

I smile, feeling accomplished. Eddie—my crush who reciprocates my feelings—is right in front of me. My genuine friend is beside me. And I too have found the toothbrush. "Got it!"

"Great!" Harold claps and comes closer to us. "Now find the item you're most attached to and hold it for a second."

I pause. Stick with the toothbrush, or go back to something else? What if we have to do a skit with the object we choose? The toothbrush will no doubt lead to issues relating to the face, and since there's no way I want to tread down that road, I quickly flick my hands around trying to find something else. Where'd that sock go?

"Find something meaningful." Harold roams the class, his voice lustrous and insistent. "When you have it, let me know."

"I'm looking," Eddie says. His voice sounds funny. Choking, almost. I look at his face but it gives nothing away. I think back to our "to be continued" conversation. To our hug.

In the dark of the box, my fingers wriggle, hoping to find the limp sock. But instead, they find something much, much better. A hand. And it's got calluses. From painting. My knuckles graze his knuckles and, just as I think it couldn't get better, his hand unfurls and grips mine. I'm holding Eddie's hand. He's holding mine. I could pass out.

I look at Eddie. His face remains blank, like during a soccer game when he's about to pass and doesn't want to give away his plan. Am I his plan?

"Have you found your object?" Harold asks.

I'm about to nod or scream or jump up and say *yes, dear world, I, Cyrie, have found my object*. The object of my affections. But I don't, because right as I open my mouth, Eddie sneezes. He lets go of me, bringing his hands out of the magical box and over his mouth and nose. Thoughtful and sanitary, and yet completely not what I'd wanted.

I wait for his hands to return to the box, which they do (after a brief swipe to his T-shirt), but they don't touch mine. It was a short-lived but wonderful pleasure.

"What do you have, Cyrie?" Harold's voice rolls over to us on the stage.

"A sock," I say, my hands roaming around for it. For some reason, this makes people crack up. Maybe it's the boredom that comes with watching other people stand around doing silly and pointless Drama exercises, or maybe it's the unspoken tension I feel standing here.

"And you, Leyla?" Harold focuses attention on her. Everyone stares.

"I . . . " Leyla swallows and nods, apparently unable to speak. For a second I think she might actually throw up. She looks so nervous, so shy (she hates speaking in class), that I'm filled with empathy for her. I give her my best *it's okay* look: a furrowed brow and an encouraging smile.

"Squeeze that thing you've found," instructs Harold. "Hold it as though it means everything to you."

I wonder what Eddie's got. A teacup? A pencil? Do any of the objects make him think of me? Does he wish his sneeze hadn't happened? I make a mental note to ask him if he has allergies. One little antihistamine and he'd still be holding my hand. Leyla still looks ill—not quite green, but off-color. Maybe she has the toothbrush. Maybe a button. Part of me feels for her, but the rest of me can't shake my

85

elation. He held my hand. And it felt right. And he wants to talk to me later.

"Did you learn something from this exercise?" Harold asks, taking his place next to us.

The three of us nod, out of habit. "Totally," Eddie says. He has a way of being sarcastic enough that kids think he's funny, but gentle enough that teachers can't call him on it.

"Definitely," Leyla mirrors. Her cheeks are bright red now and her eyes are those of a helpless kitten—if helpless kittens also looked like they were going to barf.

"Are you okay?" I ask her, but she shakes her head.

Leyla bolts from the stage and runs in the direction of the dressing rooms—no doubt to the bathroom. Eddie watches, concerned, and looks at me to see what my reaction is. I'm about to ask if I can be excused to follow Leyla, to check on her, when Harold interrupts.

"You can take your hands out of the box now, Cyrie." He raises his eyebrows. The rest of the class, except Eddie, chuckles at my expense.

I do as he says, finally bringing my hands into the light. I am more painfully aware than ever before that, outside of the dark, private box, my hands are empty.

seven

The only way to prove this night is happening and not a dream is through the incessant and temporarily blinding flash of the yearbook and *Weston Word* photographers, who are thrilled with the event. Night of Knights is in full swing, with Josh and some of his sporty cronies whacking one another with long, padded sticks, and just about every girl at Weston standing around looking maidenly in flowing pink dresses or empire-waist gowns that they think make them look like Guinevere (but in reality make them look kind of pregnant). Not that I'm one to say anything, because—for some reason in hell and much against my better judgment— I am wearing a princess dress, too.

"See? I knew you'd have fun!" Leyla clutches my arm with one hand and picks up the hem of her long, smoke-colored gown in the other. The truth is, she looks better in brighter colors, but she told me at home that she "doesn't want to stick out so much." Yeah, welcome to my world, I'd said as I slithered into the blue number I'd borrowed from my mother's stash of retro gear. The material gathers across my waist and swoops down in the back, revealing probably more skin than I've ever exposed at school, but it fits with my mood.

Exposed.

But happy. After all, drama class ended yesterday with Eddie giving me a wink and checking to make sure I'd find him later to "talk," and Leyla recovered in the girls' bathroom without too much struggle. Even though Eddie couldn't make it over to my house to talk auction, he emailed me: *Chief—looks like we need to reschedule our talk—you thinking what I'm thinking?* Which left me with palpitations and anticipation. And now we're here.

"You call this fun?" The bodice on my dress pinches my waist and I've noticed quite a few Westies staring in disbelief. Yes, folks, call a summit meeting—I'm not in sweats.

"You say that all sarcastic and everything, but the truth is, you look pretty glad you're here."

Shrugging feels appropriate about now, if only to mask what's roiling inside me. Excitement bubbles within me but I'm keeping it shoved down, dark and hidden like my hand

and Eddie's clenched in the box. "Well, it's difficult to focus with all the weirdness here."

Charging from the left of the gym, atop one of the gymnastic horses cleverly mounted on coasters, Crissy Limler leads the female jousters. She angles her rod and tries to poke at Fairlee Sykes, who everyone calls "fairly psyched" because she's generally happy all the time.

"I'm gonna get you, Fairlee!"

"Not if I get you first!"

Knights—some in rented armor, some in tinfoil garb, cheer and spill their mugs of ginger ale. The joust continues. Leyla fiddles with the flowing sleeves on her dress. She looks distracted, her eyes unable to settle on any one thing. Then again, this place is sensory-overload. "So, how come you got all pukey yesterday, anyway?" I ask.

Leyla avoids eye contact. "No reason."

"No reason? You almost chucked in class. I mean, I know you don't like public speaking and everything, but—"

Leyla frowns. "I said no reason, okay? God, you always need to know everything."

I feel as though she's pushed me, but in fact she's very still. My voice softens. "I was just asking, that's all. You know, checking on my friend?" I tilt my head and try to get her to open up. "And if I annoy you with questions, remember that I *am* a reporter."

She gives a half-hearted laugh. "True. You can't take the

nosiness out of the girl." This slips out of her mouth and then she panics. "Oh, oh, not like that. I mean, nosy like you're curious, like a newspaper person, not like you're … you know what I … "

Maybe on another night I'd lash out at her. Maybe if she were Wendy or Jill or some random PBV I'd rail on her, but right now, on this night, with Eddie's hand and our as-yet-unspoken conversation on my mind, I just pat her back. "No problem," I say. "I know what you meant."

Leyla looks relieved. She can't handle a verbal lashing any better than she can give a speech. "Anyway," she says, her eyes searching for something—or someone—in the crowd, "I was just nervous, that's all." She sees what she's looking for, and smiles. "But I'm okay now, and I'm glad you came out tonight. You won't regret it. You'll see." Her smile makes me almost believe it—that plus my inner excitement.

On the overhead speakers, a voice announces that the spectacle we've all been waiting for is about to start: the joust of nations. The school is split into "principalities." This is supposedly arbitrary, but if you look on the printout in the main corridor, the names are actually sectioned off by popularity. Suffice to say, if the nations were real, Leyla and I would require passports to enter each other's land—and mine would no doubt be revoked at the border.

Heading up one fake nation is Beef Anderson. His name

isn't really beef, but he's been called that for so long no one remembers his real name.

"Hey there, nation buddies!" Linus comes up from behind and taps me on the shoulder, all twitchy and carrying a notebook.

Leyla grabs his shoulder, glad to see him. "I'm thinking of deflecting."

Linus' eyebrows scrunch up, but his confusion is momentary. "You mean 'defecting'?"

Leyla blushes, but recovers. "Yeah—like, leave my nation and join yours."

"We'd be happy to have you," I tell her, and scan the crowd for the familiar hair ... listen for the timbre of his voice.

Linus wedges himself between my shoulder and Leyla's. "What's Beef's real name again?"

Leyla shrugs. I shake my head. "No idea. Sorry. Guess you'll have to research that for the article."

Linus stares just a little too long at me, and I recall that feeling I had before, when he said he had something to discuss with me. "Hey, Cyrie, do you think ... "

I cut him off, distracted by the dimming lights, the rising cheers. A strobe light flashes, and I know that half the people will stay to gawk at the faux brutalities of jousting and half will wander toward the dance floor. It's the time I dread. Or one of the times I dread. All the pretty girls, all the average ones, all the tall and gracious ones, all the short and perky ones—all of them dance with their noses looking normal.

Then I see him.

Eddie's eyes find mine across the floor. Does the strobe light make my face look worse? Better? Horrific, like in some creature feature? "Can we talk later, Linus? I'm kind of hating the fact that I'm here and I don't want to—"

Linus nods and writes in his notebook, sticking close by but with enough space that he doesn't get nudged by Eddie, who comes trudging toward us through the crowd. Princess girls and knightly guys back up, parting so Eddie can pass.

Leyla's eyes sweep the room and land back on Linus, who makes his exit to interview Beef for the paper. "I gotta talk to you," she whispers to me. Her hand squeezes my arm so tightly that my skin pinches.

"Ouch!" I try and pry her off while looking at Eddie. He looks—I swear—right at me and nods. My heart does an arrhythmic dance and I glance at Leyla. Did she see that? Does she care?

"Cyrie—hey," Eddie says and gives me a side-hug. It might have been a full-on body hug if only Leyla hadn't been attached to my limbs still.

"You look dashing," I say, brave and dumb at the same time, which is maybe how love (or serious like) is—more exposure.

"And you look…" Eddie takes in my gown, and has me twirl like we're in a musical. "Magnificent."

My new favorite word. In my head I do a mental thesaurus: stunning, splendid, glorious, outstanding. All good. "Thanks," I say, and feel my dress against my bare legs, the fabric soft against my skin. I think of Eddie's rough hands finding mine in Drama.

"So, Leyla, how are you this fine evening?" Eddie bows to her, ever the knightly knight, and tries to sound gallant in his Robin Hood–inspired outfit.

"I'm…" she starts to answer but then grabs me again. "I'm just a… you know, like one of those things with the way of the…"

Eddie looks amused, and then worried. "Have you been drinking?"

Leyla shakes her head. "No, I wouldn't do that." She looks to me to back her up.

"She's not drunk or anything—I mean, we got ready together, and…" Just as I'm about to explain more, Eddie puts a hand on Leyla's shoulder, trying to steady her as she starts to sway a little.

"You okay?" His eyes register concern; the corners of his mouth turn down. He looks to me as to what to do next.

"Leyla, maybe you should…" I start.

"I'm. It's. I've gotta—" Leyla bolts from the gym, tripping on her gown and ripping the bottom of it; she now appears more Cinderella-during-working-hours than at the ball. She doesn't stop until she's burst through the double doors that lead to the dark corridors of school.

Immediately, I turn to go after her. I make it to the basketball net.

"Wait, Cyrie!" Eddie's voice is insistent. I turn back. He catches up to me. "I know it's bad timing, but ... can we talk now?"

I'm torn. Be a good friend or have the talk? The talk that could lead to everything I've been wanting. I stare up at Eddie's face, his perfect mouth, his questioning eyes. "I should see if Leyla's okay," I say. Friendship trumps crush, I guess.

"Fine," Eddie nods. "You're right. Let's find her."

In our costumes, we traipse the hallways, searching. Past the cafeteria with its badly painted mural of aquatic life ("we're all in this ocean together"), past the science labs and homerooms, we repeat her name but can't find her.

"I'll check the bathrooms," I say, sure she'll resurface in a stall and that food poisoning or whatever's ailing her will give her pause by the sink. But I come out of the last bathroom holding out my hands. "Nada. She's gone."

Eddie sighs and I follow him, roaming and looking until we're outside another set of heavy double doors. He takes stock of where we are. "Hey, back to the drama of drama class."

I open the doors and look around. "Yeah, back to Harold's world."

Eddie strides down the aisle and sits on the stage, legs dangling. I join him. "It's like we're going swimming," I say, pretending to test the water with my ballet-flat-covered toes.

"Splash," Eddie says, but in a deadpan voice that makes me laugh. He laughs while I laugh. "You know, there's just not very many people I could do this with."

"Do what?" I ask. "We're not doing anything."

Eddie shrugs. "I know, but that's my point. Make up stuff with, or just sit on the stage and mime with."

"Miming is silent. We were doing improv." I notice our thighs are nearly touching. "Nice tights, by the way."

He doesn't pause, but plucks a bit of stretchy fabric away from his leg. "Yeah, I'm going for studly but kind, Robin-Hood-meets-action-adventure-hero." He clears his throat and adjusts his position so one leg still dangles but the other is up on stage, touching mine. We're only inches apart. "I'm serious, though. You know we have something special, right?"

Magnificent. Special. This is it. These are the words I've been waiting for, the ones that change everything. "We do." I meet his gaze. We're going to kiss. We're going to be a couple. We'll go to the prom and hold hands in the halls and kiss by the ugly dumb aquatic mural in the cafeteria with the stench of dry meatloaf wafting all around us.

"And so . . . " Eddie licks his lips. "I feel like I can confide in you." He waits for my reaction. I nod. Go on, confide.

"And I can do the same with you," I finally say, encouraging him, wanting to draw this moment out so I can remember it exactly as it happens as I try to fall asleep tonight.

"So, you probably can tell, then, about my ... um ... " He uses his Harold-drama voice: "Feelings."

I act back, my voice overly deep. "Your feelings? Do explain."

Eddie drums his fingers on his leg and hops down from the stage so that he's right between my knees. A bit awkward for kissing, but not terrible. His voice goes back to normal, but waivers. "I like her so much, Cyrie."

He's so tongue-tied he uses the wrong pronoun. I love it. "Yeah ... "

"And do you think she likes me?" His face pleads with me, his eyes desperate for an answer.

"I think *she* does, yes." I make the pronoun joke back to him, but he doesn't seem to get it.

"God, what a relief. I mean, I thought so, but she's hard to read, you know? If only I knew her better."

I feel confusion rumbling inside me. I draw my legs up to my chest and pull my dress down to cover myself; I'm tucked into a ball. "But—you do know me."

Eddie smiles and looks distracted. "I know *you*, of course I do. If only she were as easy to get to know, you know? Damn, that was a bad sentence." He shoves his hands into his pockets.

Feeling as though the floor might not be there to meet me, I jump from the stage and try to get my bearings. I sit in one of the theater seats and Eddie sits in the row in front of me, facing away from me like we're both watching the show.

"So," I say swallowing. "What is it, exactly, that you want to tell me?"

"I thought for sure you'd know by now, given your reporter tendencies," Eddie says. "But since you claim to be in the dark . . . " In the dark where our hands met. In the dark where I was more sure of everything. "But I never thought I'd find someone so . . . sweet, you know?" I'm sweet. "So fun and fun to be with." Also me. "So open to trying new things and just kind of out there, you know?" I do know, because that's me. "Who kind of electrifies me, for lack of a better word." I want to suggest "excites" or "thrills" or "amazes" as alternatives to "electrify," but I don't because right as I'm opening my mouth, Eddie says, "And so, so pretty."

"Is that how you see her?" I ask. Gathering all my guts, I lean forward and touch his shoulder. He tips his head back to see me. "It's true, then, all those myths about someone's exterior not being the most important thing?" Instinct takes over and I touch my nose, the whole length of it, and I don't curse it. I don't think about chopping it off.

Eddie sits up and wrinkles his brow. "No, it's totally important. I mean, I'm not the only one. Empirically, she's hot. No one could argue that." His eyes meet mine.

And just like that, the floor sinks away. The stage recedes. We are watching a show, only it's not *Romeo and Juliet*, it's not *Guys and Dolls*. It's one where the girl does not get the guy she wants. My hand withdraws from his shoulder. He's not describing me. He is talking about—

"Leyla." His face lights up. "She's awesome."

My heart stammers, but my words stay intact. "She is. She certainly is." I pause. "And really, um..." My voice falters. "Really pretty, as you say." I want to cry, not just out of disappointment but because I feel so lame. Why would he want me, when he could have her?

"I need to get going, actually," I say and stand up. I'm suddenly exhausted, but it's going to take lots of list-making or college essays to make me bored enough to go to sleep tonight.

"Wait—the thing is this, Cyr..." Eddie flicks my shoulder: the ultimate in *just friends*. "She's so shy, you know? And I really want to hang out with her but she kind of..."

I get it. All her nerves, her near-vomitous episodes. "She bolts. Yeah. She's..." I could tell him to forget it. Say that she likes someone else, or that she doesn't like him, or that being around him makes her feel ill. But instead I just say, "She's just nervous, is all." I look at his face. The same face, attached to the same boy, attached to the same wit and smarts and charm that I've crushed on for so long. I should write crappy love songs. Then pretty girls could burn them onto mixes for guys who like them back. "What exactly do you want me to do?"

"I know *about* her but I don't really know *her*, if you get what I'm saying."

My lips are dry and chapped from the stale Drama air, and my heart feels worse. "You want to find out her innermost thoughts and all her intimate details?" I paraphrase "Somebody," a Depeche Mode song I downloaded only days ago.

"Exactly." Eddie slings one of his killer smiles my way, his eyes crinkling on the sides. "Think you could talk to her for me? School's kind of busy and there are so many people." He rubs his hands together. "Maybe see if she wants to hang out or talk on the phone or something?"

I pull my arms around my over-exposed self and nod. "Sure," I say and feel a chill wash over my skin. "No harm in asking."

eight

"I'm all done, I think," Leyla yells from her bathroom. I'm sitting at her desk waiting for her to emerge from yet another round of the nervous heaves.

She appears in front of me in boy-cut bottoms and a flannel pajama top, every inch the sweet and pretty girl Eddie described. "I just can't believe he—Rox—likes me! Oh God, I might do it again." She holds her stomach. Then she shakes it off. "No. I'm good." She grins and flips her hair out of her face, securing it in a loose knot. "I can't believe this! Tell me again."

I've already told her, what feels like a dozen times, about my conversation with Eddie—about how much he likes her, about all the words he used to describe her. I did not include my miserable feelings—my letdown that caused me to stay up until the sun rose, wondering why I can't get the damn nose job sooner than my birthday and wishing I'd never liked Eddie in the first place. "I've told you enough now," I say and use one of her multi-colored flower pens as a drum stick on her desk. I tap some tune that only makes sense to me and then ask, "So, what should I tell him?"

"Tell him yes. Absolutely." Leyla goes to her closet and starts flinging through potential Monday morning outfits. "How do I look in green? No. Blue."

"Leyla?" I watch her hold up a sundress, a skirt, a faded top. "How exactly are you planning on being near him without … you know … losing it?"

Leyla's face is crestfallen. She stops touching clothing and sits in a heap on the floor. "I know. I know! That's the thing. It'll never happen. He wants to get to know the 'inside of me' as you said, but I seriously doubt that means getting to know *the inside of me*." She points to her stomach.

"You'll be fine. Just take Dramamine or something."

"Drama class isn't going to help me," Leyla says.

"Drama-mine," I say slowly. "It's an anti-emetic." Cue the blank look from Leyla. "Hyperemesis is when you throw up too much. That's kind of what you have. Dramamine is a medicine that—"

Leyla lies flat on the rug, flailing her arms. "Nope. Not

that. It's so not even an issue about the puking, even though of course that's not a plus. It's like ... "

I can't believe I'm here listening to my friend blather on about the guy she likes, who is really the guy I like—but here I am. So I do what any good friend would do. I listen and try to act the way I would if this didn't involve Eddie. "So what's the main problem?"

"He likes this ... " She waves her hand over her face and body like someone displaying a new car. "But what about this?" She points to her head.

"Your hair?" I touch her thick locks.

"No." She sits up and frowns. "I mean the brain thing on the inside."

"The 'brain thing'?" I can't help but laugh.

"God, why are you such a nitpicker? Fine. My brain. It's just, like, Rox is so ... "

"Intellectual?" I offer and wish I hadn't said the "brain thing" comment. It's just I can't help it. Sometimes the words just rush out, like water breaking free of a dam.

"Smart, yeah. And he knows so much and here I am not even knowing that dramadedine is for throwing up."

"Dramamine." Automatically, I correct her.

"Cyrie, come on!"

"Sorry—we used to go sailing a lot and I was the queen of nausea ... " I stop short, remembering feeling decidedly unqueenlike at Night of Knights with Eddie.

Leyla undoes the knot of her hair and looks unkempt and gorgeous as she rolls onto her stomach. She reaches under her bed and pulls out a dusty yearbook and flips to the candids section. The same section I've stared at for far too long. And for what? So I can facilitate someone else's coupledom.

She points to Eddie. "He's got everything. The outside and the inside."

"You do, too," I insist. "I mean it." She looks doubtful. "Even if I correct you."

She pauses, thinking of something. "That's right. You do correct me."

I nod, feeling bad. "I'm working on it, what can I say? It's a fault."

"No, it's not a bad thing. Not always..." Leyla's voice holds excitement now. She sits up, her eyes flashing. "In fact, it's a great thing!"

"What do you mean?" I watch her flit around her room. She goes to her closet and then sits down, then she paces and then, finally, she gets her laptop and slides it between us on the rug. "What?"

Leyla claps her hands, still a cheerleader. "You edit me, right? I mean, you do it all the time at the *Word*. Like that story on lunches and the removal of the soda machines? You were great!"

"Well, thanks, I guess, even if it's a little bit irrelevant." I shrug. She can be so random.

Leyla continues, her words fast. "You always know what to say. And I want to sound great with Rox, you know, get him to like me more, but . . . " She searches for the best words. "But, like, the best version of me."

"Leyla, what're you saying?" I sit cross-legged, wondering where this is leading. She opens her laptop and I hear the familiar start-up music.

"What I'm saying is that he wants to get to know me, but how am I supposed to believe he really just wants to talk, instead of 'talk'?" She does air quotes, then explains. "Ogling my boobs or something?"

"Leyla . . . believe it or not, I do know what 'talking' is." I give her a wry smile. "I mean, I do watch movies." Fine, so I haven't been to a party where a guy asks me to take a "walk" so we can "talk." But still.

"No, it's true, Cyr. Guys in the past—Josh, for one— only wanted to be with me for my looks." She pushes her hair away from her face, her cheeks rosy with whatever idea she's hatching. "So fine, Rox seems like he's different, and I want him to prove it. So, we don't meet in person, and I don't puke."

For once, I'm the slow one. "I'm not following you." Leyla types into the computer and grins.

"Wait . . . okay, let me explain." She turns the screen to face me. On the screen she's started an email to Eddie but left a few words blank, like a Mad Lib. I suddenly click in to what she's getting at.

"Whoa…no, wait a second, Leyla." I hold my hands out like a stop sign.

"It's perfect, don't you see? I email him—real emails, not IMs, and you…"

"I proofread them for clarity?" My nerves are starting to prickle, doubt creeping in. It's one thing to talk to Leyla for Eddie, and another to support her—but something else entirely to be privy to their courtship.

Leyla tilts her head back and forth. "Not exactly. You know how sometimes I use the wrong word? Or, maybe if I say something dumb…" She looks at me with her eyebrows raised as question marks.

"No way."

"Okay, okay, okay. You won't pick the words." She looks at me and I sigh with relief. Then she starts up again. "Then just edit me—not for content, just for spelling and stuff."

"You have spellcheck."

"But that doesn't always work—you know, 'theirs' versus 'there's,' and 'your' and 'you're'…" She waits, tapping her long fingers on her knee.

"Just Dramamine, not dramadenine? Stuff like that?" I ask. She nods at me. I stand up, circling the room and wondering what I'm getting myself into. "So it's not anything dishonest, right? I just clean up your prose."

Leyla stands and hugs me. "Exactly. A comma here…"

"A semicolon there." My stomach does its own twists

and turns. I'm up for editor of the year—it's a big contest all across New England; just to be nominated means you've got the right to think of yourself as great in that arena. I am a good editor. And wouldn't this be the ultimate test of that? If I can edit impartially? "But we don't tell Eddie?"

Leyla's smile freezes. "Never. He'll get to know me through emails, and then when we're really, you know, close, he won't care that I don't know the difference between geography and geology."

I make a face. "You do, too."

Leyla grins. "Only kinda. But the point is, you swear you won't ever tell him about this, right?"

I nod. My brain then goes into editorial mode: logistics and time management. "If I have to come over here or be with you every time you email, this will take forever. Ideally, you should be able to blip things off to him multiple times a day. So..."

"So, I could give you my password?" Leyla offers, going back to her computer.

I stop her. There's close friends and then there's too close. "I'm not sure I should have that—you know, with test scores and other emails..." She looks dejected. She's so willing and open, like an animated fawn or something you want to take care of. Maybe that's part of her appeal, and what I'm lacking. "But I have a solution."

"Phew. I got worried there." She breathes a sigh of relief and waits for me to solve the problem.

I bite a cuticle as I explain. "We create a new account. An email that's only for this. No e-tail shopping, no chitchat, no other conversations. Only between you and Eddie." Her and Eddie. My fist clenches automatically but I force it open.

"Rox."

"Eddie."

Leyla gives me a pointed look. "I call him Rox and you can't edit that."

"No," I say, the gravity of this arrangement settling in, "I can't."

Leyla types and clicks and types and clicks and then, "Viola!"

"I think you mean, *voilà!*"

"It's not viola?" She looks confused and mouths the word to herself a few times.

"Viola is the instrument, like a violin. And *voilà* is the French expression, 'here it is.'" I stare at the screen in front of us. "Now we just need a screen name."

"What do you think about 'Got Me on My Knees'? You know, like that Eric Clapton song, 'Layla'? Like me, get it?"

"Too sexual." Editor Cyrie jumps in. "You want something fun but romantic. A name that gets at why you're doing this." I think about how Leyla has, in the past, forgotten codes and files. Last year we couldn't locate the layout document until she remembered she'd filed it under "out." I think back to sitting on the stage with Eddie, how wrong I was about him liking me.

Then I think about that song I quoted to him by Depeche Mode. It wouldn't make my top ten from the '80s, but it's all about looking for—wanting—that perfect fit with someone. *Innermost thoughts and intimate details* is too long for a screen name, but what about, "Somebody@gmail.com?"

"Taken." Leyla shakes her head as she types. "Next?"

"Sum-bo-dee," I suggest, spelling it out.

"Clever," she says, testing the address. "Yup, it works. Password should be . . . ?" She looks up at me through the curtain of her hair. "Rox?"

"Eddie?" I counter, smirking. I check my watch. Essays are calling me, as is my article about the school budget, and, yes, prep for my auction-brainstorming session with Eddie tomorrow. Plus, I have to factor in time to mope. All my dreams of crushes working out, of being asked to dance, of going for a "walk" to "talk" with Eddie have been dashed, and it'll take awhile to recover. I stand up, feeling my legs ache. My heart thuds. Are we really doing this? Am I?

"How about just Cyrie?" Leyla suggests.

"But it's *your* account." I walk to her bedroom door and wait for her answer.

"But using my name's too obvious. Besides, the longer it

takes for me to think of this and set it up, the more I feel like chickening out." She crosses her arms. "Please?"

"Fine. Use Cyrie. But I have to go." I bite my lip, wishing she were the one helping *me* land the guy. That misogynistic fairy tales and pointless myths really added up to the right girl getting what she wants. Then I realize maybe Leyla is the right girl, even if she doesn't know what misogynistic means.

She enters my name. "Okay. But tell me again how this is gonna work. I don't want to get my wires crossed."

I put my hands on my hips. Life would be easier if I could just organize everything and have it turn out the way I want it to. The sunlight streams through Leyla's window and, across the rug, shadows form—including a long, awkward one. My profile. No matter where I go, I wind up back here.

"I seriously have to go, but here's the deal: you write an email and save it in your Sumbodee account as a draft. I log on, sign in and check it, make any changes like messed-up words or commas, and then I send it to Rox."

Leyla snaps her fingers. "Simple as that!"

The room seems like it's a snow globe, nice and neat and settled and pristine—with a pretty girl on the floor with her laptop that will lead to love. I nod, through tears that spring up unexpectedly in my eyes. "Yeah, simple," I say blurring the image and feeling the longing spread inside me. I push it back down, pack it away like old clothing I need to give away. "Easy."

nine

In a million years, I never would have pictured Eddie in a bonnet and Bo Peep–style skirt. But the sad truth of the matter is that even in weird drag, he still looks hot. "Am I a catch or what?" he asks me as he tries to maneuver the hoop skirt and sip his beverage at the same time.

Any Time Now is in full swing, tables filled with Weston's lesser-knowns, the fringe crowd and the drama-mamas who are busy belting out High School Musical tunes and then switching to Sondheim. Eddie and I have my favorite table, and I try my very hardest not to feel a thing as he offers to share a heart-shaped scone. My appetite isn't hearty, since I've got a nervous stomach from explaining the email scheme to him: Leyla's account, the no-pressure way of "talking." I just left out the part about my role in the whole thing.

"Seriously, I'm hot in this, right?" Eddie tilts his bonnet toward me.

"Sure, you're a catch," I say in my best sarcastic voice. "Real appealing in frills." I flick his bonnet. "But back to work." I point to our list of auction items. We've separated them into categories. "We've got possible, potential, and probable. Too many in the potentials—we need more sure things."

Tell me about it, I think, and allow myself one short-lived gaze. Just a moment of wistful thinking. I shake it off.

"Well, you got the Von Schmedler's place, so that's a biggie." Eddie breaks off a piece of scone and eats it, thinking. "Any other ideas?"

I wave to Hanna Fisher, who's busy serving tea sandwiches while showcasing her lace-up Victorian boots. "I'm in!" she yells, miming money with her fingers.

"Write that one down," I say and watch Eddie write, wondering if and when he's going to ask about Leyla again. "Hanna's giving this place out for a graduation party. That should get some funds."

Eddie nods. "We've got sporting goods, gift certificates from some places in town. I scored tux rentals—could be good for the prom. And Plumpy's Candies donated a massive basket of all things promoting tooth decay." He looks at me and hands me a piece of scone. "What's your candy of choice, by the way?"

"Malted milkballs, spearmint leaves, chocolate licorice, Snowcaps. Not in that order," I say, as though I planned it out. I can think very quickly on my feet—or nose.

"I highly approve," Eddie says. "I'm a milkball man myself." He grins. "Did that sound dirty, or is it just me?"

I laugh—the pleasure of joking, edged with hurt from knowing it won't lead anywhere. Like when my mother bought me a bag of spearmint leaves right after I had my wisdom teeth pulled—look but don't touch. I sip my tea. "We should ask around at the hardware store..."

"Already have it." He taps his pen, then chews the cap.

"Bender's Ice Cream," I suggest. He writes it down. "Faye's Nail Emporium."

"Ellie's Books," he adds. "WNPS radio—maybe they'll do a personalized show or something."

"Now you're thinking," I say and feel that rush of being with him. The ease, the natural flow of ideas. The two of us leaning over the table, near enough to... never mind. "Samasa's Restaurant. Add that. They do those gourmet picnic baskets."

"Samasa's... got it..." Eddie writes down my suggestions without the pen pausing on the paper. He's talking with his mouth full of scone, which should be gross but instead is charming. "And so, with the whole email thing you told me about—when do you think she'll send one?"

I grimace. Ooops. Subliminal sublimation, maybe. Leyla called and told me to proof her first email, but I never did. And never sent it.

"Um, soon," I say. "I'm sure it'll be soon." I dig my fingernails into my palm, wishing I didn't know all about this— except part of me is glad I do. For one thing, I'm a snoop. Another thing is that somehow, the more I know about something—a situation, a book, an event—the more in control I feel. So even though I am sure this is out of my hands—I mean, you can't *make* someone desire you—I'm still kind of connected to it. To him. I look at his hair, his hands on the page, the doodle he's making. Wordlessly, I take the pen and add to the doodle and we sit like that, in quiet comfort, sharing a scone and making aimless art together.

The whole scene is quite lovely until the front door opens and a waft of evil comes right toward us.

"I see you've decided to ignore fashion advice once again, Cyrie." Jill Carnegie folds her arms over her methodically layered outfit and gives me the once-over.

I smooth the ruffles of my pirate shirt, feeling not quite as cool and fun as a minute before. Somehow, with Eddie in a skirt and me in a fluffy white top reminiscent of a high seas adventure, we are not the image of domestic bliss I have in my mind. "It's called a costume, Jill, and it wouldn't hurt you to break free of your drone mode and try it on."

"Yeah," Eddie challenges. He's good-humored about it, offering his bonnet to her. She keeps her arms and hands away from it as though it's diseased.

"Um, no thank you." Jill studies my face. "And, ew."

"I'm sure the bonnet's thinking the same thing," I say. I can see her eyeing my nose, see the slagging off about to start. Eddie shoots me a look as though what I've just said is uncalled for. "What do you want, Jill?"

"None of your business," Jill says, and faces Eddie.

"She's cool, Jill." With his hat off, Eddie looks more normal, and I feel slightly foolish in my get-up.

Jill snickers. "Whatever. All I came to tell you is that you're late for Wendy's..." She looks at me. "You know..."

Eddie looks blank for a minute, then nods. "Oh, yeah." He looks at me. "You wanna come? It's just a get-together at her house. No big thing." He ignores Jill's huffy foot stomp, her head shake.

I don't want to go, but I like to see Eddie stand up for me and I like seeing Jill sweat it out. Wendy Von Meanie would not be pleased with her minions if they showed up with me in tow. "Well, it's not like I have much else to do today..." Jill looks strained and Eddie shrugs. "But no."

"Oh, thank God," Jill says and swivels to leave, tugging Eddie along with her.

"You okay?" Eddie asks. His face shows true concern, but his feet are pointed toward the door.

"Sure. Go have fun with the toddler set."

Eddie's brow furrows. "Don't be mean, Cyrie."

"I'm not," I say and want to defend myself with all the years of torment they've dumped on me, but Eddie puts some money on the table.

"As always, a pleasure to hang out with you," he says, sliding out of his skirt and hanging it back on the coat rack. I watch him and look at our list, at our collaborative doodle. Amidst the lines and circles, the jagged pen marks, he's drawn a heart. Not a perfect one, one that slants off to the side, right near me—except aimed for someone else.

The next morning at home, I think about Eddie and then about Leyla's unsent message. I should proof it. I close my door, ignoring the fresh French toast and syrup my dad left for me, and check the email account. Leyla's first email is still safe. Nothing big, nothing noteworthy, just an introduction, really. I fill my lungs to capacity, semi-disbelieving I'm actually going to do this. I set the account to save all the messages that are sent and click on the first one. Leyla writes:

Hi Rox—

*Your not going to believe this but I'm ner-
vous typing! How do you like this idea of
sending messages? It'll be pretty cool once we
get into it. Don't you think?*

Write me soon.

Leyla

I clean up the your/you're situation, put a comma in, and then send it off. It's not the intro I would have used—I mean, it hardly grabs your (or you're, heh) attention—but it's fine. I gather my school stuff together and put it into my bag, take a few bites of toast, change my shirt after I spill syrup on it, and just when I'm about to leave, the computer alerts me to a new message.

L—

*Two messages in one morning! Looks like my
lucky day. I was waiting to hear from you and
wondering if maybe you were reconsidering
this correspondence. That's what it is—or will
be—isn't it? Just like in the old days when
people actually sat there in cafes and wrote letters or postcards and had to wait for responses.
That's what this will be, only we can still see*

*each other in school. I can't wait to write more
but I just realized I have no clean socks and I
don't want to offend you with any potential
smell at the Word meeting today.*

More soon—

Rox

*P.S. Not sure which email I should reply
to...?*

Two emails? I call Leyla, my heart racing, my breakfast lodged in my throat.

"Hey," I say into the phone. I'm frustrated that she can't follow even the simplest of instructions, and my tone indicates this. "What're you doing sending him an email?"

Leyla lets out a semi-snort. "Um, excuse me?"

"He just wrote back, saying you sent two messages."

"I only sent one," Leyla insists.

"But I sent the one you sent to our account," I explain, still focused on the screen.

"*My* account?"

I shake my head, annoyed. "Leyla. We agreed you'd send mail from the Sumbodee account, right?"

Leyla makes a noise that sounds like a strangled fish. "Uhagaga... sorry! I got impatient and thought you weren't doing your thing, you know, sending the email. So I sent one from my regular account. Is that bad?"

Her voice is sweet, not whiney, and I can imagine her placid eyes and worried brow. I sigh. Why do I get so worked up? Just editorial instinct. I bite my lip. "It's not great, but it's not the end of the world. Look, don't write to him from your account. Go into the Sumbodee one now and fire off a quick thing—and make sure to explain that this is your real account. The one he should use. Okay?"

Leyla screams, "Just a second!" Then, in a regular voice, she tells me, "Sorry, that wasn't for you . . . " The decibel level jumps again. "Give! Me! One! Minute!" She's really riled up; no doubt her dad is forcing her off the line.

"Okay?" I check my own watch and heft my backpack on. Inside are my books, essays, and running shoes. I have a pre-op appointment with Dr. Singer today (or, as I think of him, Dr. Schnoz), and figure that if I'm not playing varsity anymore I should at least give myself some cardio and jog there from school. "Time to go."

"No. Wait. Cyrie?" Leyla shuffles things on her end. "My dad's going to kill me if I take more time this morning doing computer stuff."

I hold the phone with my chin, sweep my hair into a ponytail, and get annoyed all over again. "Leyla, do you want this or not?"

"I do! Just please—you send something back—a little

thing that just buys me time until study hall this afternoon when I can write more. Please?"

I want to point out that this is dishonest. That this isn't what we should be doing. That she should conduct this back-and-forth herself. But I hear the desperation in her voice and just say, "Okay. But only this once and then it's all you."

"Awesome. Thanks!" She hangs up.

I reread what he's written. Correspondence. My fingers tingle on the keys.

Immediately, I want to write about how I've always wanted an old-fashioned courtship by letter. A paper-and-pen collection of missives that I bind together with ribbon and pass down to my children. And I want to crack a joke about his smelly socks, about how I remember that last year he turned a pair inside out and wore them as though that would do anything for the stench.

"You're going to be late!" my mom yells up the stairs.

"I'm coming!" I type.

Hey You—

Sorry for the confusion before. Just use this address. The other one's filled with spam and I hardly check it. Hope your morning is off to a good start. See you later!

Leyla

I almost end it there but then tack on my real thoughts:

> *Wouldn't the world be a better place if people still wrote letters? Real ones with pens or quills and fine paper? Or even a ballpoint and a legal pad? Looking forward to seeing you.*

I figure it's the truth—at least from my point of view—and it spices up the letter enough to make him want to write back. I press *send* and log out of the account. Words flutter into my mind like butterflies and falling autumn leaves. Tons of words. But nowhere to put them.

ten

$\mathcal{T}$ime ticks away, bringing me closer to Dr. Schnoz. I study the page in front of me on which I have started—yet again—my essay about my greatest flaw being my greatest strength. Watching Eddie watch Leyla, who is sitting next to me in study hall, I know that nothing will come to me on this topic because right now it feels like a bunch of BS.

Last night, as I told my mom about the variety of auction items gleaned around town, she smiled and, ignoring my victories, went for my Achilles heel. "But what about you?" she asked, stressing the *you* while my dad handed her a mug of hot cocoa. I felt like I was trapped in drama class when we had to purposefully act badly, in order to illustrate good acting.

"I'm fine," I said. "Did you miss the part about me and my multiple auction items? I'm leading the way for the entire *Weston Word* staff."

"What your mother means..." my dad said, and then my mother elbowed him in the side and spilled her drink.

"Don't speak for me," she said, her voice happy and playful. Her pet peeve is when people talk for her.

"Fine," Dad clarified. "What I feel is that you are—in your words—rocking the auction. However..." (cue exchange of parental looks) "...it just feels as though you're walking around in a daze. A little distracted."

I had to hand it to them—as lame as their techniques are for getting me to spew my feelings, they at least can recognize my brain's inability to focus right now. It's not school, not sports, not the intense college pressures or prioritizing of work and the paper. It's just Eddie. All the energy I'd put into liking him is still with me, only it's got nowhere to go. All those words that swarmed in my head at Leyla's are still there, nagging me and knowing they have to stay bottled inside.

"I could be a little distracted," I ceded. "But not in a major way. Nothing to be—you know—concerned about."

They looked relieved. No pit of drugs and despair, à la formerly hot bands who spiral downward and wind up working the late shift at Gas 'n Sip or counting hangers at the dry cleaners. "Well, if you need to talk..." my mother offered. She sipped her drink.

Dad touched my cheek and then the tip of my nose. "Hey—you didn't flinch!" He notes this as progress of some kind.

"I'm too distracted to flinch," I joked.

"You know the cure for distraction?" Mom asked with her eyes back on her charts and graphs for work. I raised my eyebrows. "Action."

The paper in front of me remains blank as I flick my pen around and wonder why the hell seniors have study hall anyway. We should be excused from any and all requirements like this. "We shouldn't be here," I whisper to Leyla.

She dodges a wad of paper from Wendy and nods at me. "Maybe you could write an exposé about it."

Resting my head on my desk, I shrug. "Yeah, the cruelties of study hall and the truth about why we're here."

"I know why I'm here," she says. She points to her computer screen and asks what I think.

Rox—as in Roxy Music. Do you like that band? They were way popular back in the late 70s and I think they rock even though they're not a rock band really. There's a song they sing called Oh Yeah and it's really pretty. What music do you like? I wish I could be at

the beach right now but I'm stuck in study
hall!!!

"So, what do you think?" She nudges me and I nudge her back but don't make eye contact.

"It's fine." I reach for ChapStick and slide it on, wondering what Wendy's note says. Leyla has it still balled up on her lap. "Open your note."

"I will. But really, do you think he'll like it?"

If she'd asked anything else I could have glossed over it. If, for example, she'd said *are there spelling errors?* or, *does this sound reasonable?* I could have said no, or sure, and left it at that.

"Do I think he'll like it?" Leyla nods. I shake my head. "Um, truthfully? Not really."

She looks disappointed, but surprisingly okay. "I kind of figured it sucked."

I turn to face her. "So, what're you going to do now?"

She thinks a minute. "It's not entirely bad, you know? It's just, I'm over-thinking it all. It should flow better. Isn't that what you're always telling Linus and everyone?" As if he heard his name across the room, Linus waves to us from by the windows. He's busy writing something, too. Maybe study hall isn't so bad if you can actually accomplish things.

"Look," I tell her. "I can't write my essay and you don't see me freaking out, do you?"

Leyla tilts her head. "You're not freaking out, but you're not your usual witty self."

"Point taken." She's onto something there, I have to admit. All the strength I'm using to bottle up my Eddieness and my flock of words is tiring. I feel more drained than inspired. I sigh. "Look, sometimes you have to wait for inspiration."

Leyla reflects and furrows her brow. "I thought you told me once that you can't wait for inspiration—you have to make it."

"Did I say that?" I ask, and watch as the man himself strides into study hall. Eddie is in his worn-in blue sweatshirt, so frayed that the zipper's broken—which I know only because he lent it to me last year when we had a freak snowfall in April and I'd only worn a T-shirt to school. I'd felt cloaked in him when I borrowed it, and even though I didn't go so far as to sleep in it, I wished I had.

"So maybe you do need to make things happen." I study her email again. "Like, when you talk about Roxy Music, you could mention the lyrics you like. You tell him the song you like but you don't say why. Or you don't mention what's so great about the beach. If you want him to know you, you have to let him know you."

Leyla listens to me, hears me, transfixed. "You're so right." She bites her top lip. "You do it."

The words swarm in me. I know what she should write, what she should say. What Eddie wants from her. "No."

"Just this last time. Then I can see how you do it and go from there."

Across the room, Eddie laughs at something, and I watch him as he's reprimanded. His hand felt so good on mine in the Drama box. Just the way hands should feel. "Fine. But this is the last time."

"Just edit what I wrote here, and maybe add in something funny."

"You're funny yourself," I say, watching Leyla ignore the note from Wendy.

"But not on paper. You have to be smart to be funny with words. I'm funny like this." Leyla makes a weird face, pulling her mouth apart with her fingers and looking as ghastly as she can.

I crack up. Even if she hasn't got a way with words, I'm so glad she's my friend. That I can help her. "Go like that for Halloween, okay?"

"Aren't we a bit old for trick-or-treating?" she asks.

"Aren't you a bit old to have me writing things for you?"

Leyla winces. "You're so cutting sometimes." She blushes, looking at Eddie then back at me. She flings the note at me and I read it. "Come to Wendy's party with me," she says. "Look, in case you can't deal with another night of costumes, dressing up is optional."

I fold the note and hand it back. "Von Schmuckler? No thanks."

"You know you want to." Leyla eggs me on. "We'll see who dresses the sluttiest, okay? Test your … hypothe …"

"My hypothesis? You mean, that the girls with the lowest self-esteem need to bare the most cleavage?" I look at Eddie and his cronies. He'll be at the party. And being with Leyla is fun. Plus, I'm supposed to be doing all the senior year stuff. "Fine—but no costume for me."

Leyla nods. "Sure thing." She gathers her stuff together and eyes the computer again. "So you'll do it?" I nod hesitantly. "And I like the beach because … it's just … so fun!"

She squeezes my arm as a goodbye and goes to join Wendy and her clan of cave dwellers for a pilgrimage to the mall a few towns over. The rest of the students filter out, the jumble of bodies and colors and bits of conversations like confetti around me. Wordlessly, Linus signals to me and signs *look down*. I half expect to find my shirt stained or badly buttoned, but instead there's an airplane by my desk. Had a paper plane really flown over my head and I hadn't noticed? I really am distracted. I nod at Linus and slip the note into my pocket for later. With the big study room finally quiet and nearly empty, I use the few remaining minutes I have before my run to the doctor's office.

Rox—

Did you know you have a band that's semi-named after you? Roxy Music. Bryan Ferry is the front man, or was—who knows what he does now. He wore a suit and looked very dapper on the cover of some album I found in a second-hand store. Anyway, my favorite song is "Oh, Yeah." It's kind of depressing—I believe a breakup is happening in it—but it's so pretty and so well written. The music echoes the meaning of the words; the mark of great songwriting talent, I think.

This is all a long-winded way of saying—do you want to be Rox? Or Eddie? Do you feel as though they're the same person or that somehow since your moniker stuck so early that you've somehow become a split person?

I sometimes I feel split—like there's one side of me that's . . .

I stop. One side of Leyla. Not me. I think of how to sum her up and still sound real.

There's one side of me that everyone thinks they know, and another part that maybe only a couple people really see. Sometimes I wish I could just be both at the same time, but then I also like keeping a section of my mind that's only for me. Does that make sense? I listened to you in the Word meeting and sat there wondering if anyone else noticed the way you use the word "however" a lot. It's a funny word to slip into places, and maybe you'll think it's lame that I noticed this peculiar literary trait of yours, but there you go. Often I think that these little noticings (for lack of a better word) are what makes a person unique. HOWEVER (poking fun at me, not you), maybe this is just a lot of study hall-induced babble.

Leyla

eleven

My feet pound the pavement, revoltingly awful music from the mix I made for Leyla (*Songs You Didn't Know Could Be So Bad*) playing in my ears. The soles of my well-worn sneakers hit the leaf-strewn sidewalk and Eddie's reply resounds in me:

> *Leyla—*
>
> *You surprise me with your candor. You seem guarded at our Word meetings—HOW-EVER—on the page the lines just read really naturally. It's what we in the newspaper industry call "good flow." However, I could*

be making that up. However, it sounds okay. However, I am kind of loving the fact that you noticed my affinity for this word.

And yes, I do feel the Two Halves of Eddie situation. Rox is the school one, who is me but who is also a lot of things people want me to be or think that I am, and Eddie is my parents and my sister and my little brother and regular sitting at home me. And maybe one friend or two. And maybe you?

I'd love to write more; HOWEVER, I cannot. I have soccer practice, loads of homework, yet another round of edits from Cyrie on the article I started last week, and now a dumb costume to throw together for Von Schmedler's shindig (and no I don't usually use the word shindig, HOWEVER, I like it here—kinda retro and aware of itself at the same time).

Googled that song "Oh Yeah" and will download it tonight. I'm always game for new music (or old new music) so fire some more my way, even if they are not named after me. Write soon—

Rox (AKA Eddie)

I jog past the bank with its sturdy brick walls, past the town hall all stout and set back from the road by its semi-circular driveway, past Any Time Now with its windows shut and covered as Hanna prepares a new time period, and all along the roads I've jogged on so many times—by myself, with teammates, with Sarah Jensen and her perfectly pristine white shoes and double-knotted laces. But today, it's different. I'm lighter somehow. Happier? Not really, but it's as though the words that leaked onto the page (or screen) to Eddie today calmed me. All that built-up tension and muddle churned out one little email and made me feel better. And he wrote back. Fast.

The waiting room at Dr. Schnoz's office is lined with uncomfortable, high-backed chairs and a green couch set with plump needlepoint pillows. Upon closer inspection, the needlework isn't just designs and roses, but words, phrases: *A nose by any other name, A nose knows,* and so on. Is this supposed to be funny? I look around to see if anyone else cares. A woman with a bandage on her face reads a magazine that displays last summer's offerings, instead of anything timely. A kid and his grandfather take turns with tic-tac-toe.

How come I never noticed the pillows before? Are they new? Did I not care before, or overlook them because my parents were with me? They'd sat and worried as I went in for my initial consultation, then looked relieved when the appointment ended with the doctor assuring them I had "all the time in the world to think about this big decision." It's big all right. I wipe my forehead and blow my nose with one of the tissues from the multitude of boxes thoughtfully placed around the room.

I sit down, removing the unfunny pillows from behind my back, and script a response to Eddie's email in my mind. There are so many songs to tell him about. He would love Leon Russell and LL Cool J and Radiohead's first album (maybe he knows it, but maybe he only knows their latest album ...). I take out my notebook to write down things to tell him—things to ask him—and then, right when I'm about to stop myself because, really, that was my last email to him anyway, I feel something poking my thigh.

I rummage in my pocket and pull out the now-folded paper-airplane note from Linus. In his familiar block printing, neat and square and solid, he's written:

WE NEVER GOT A CHANCE TO TALK. NEVER SEEMS TO BE A GOOD TIME. WE GO WAY BACK, YOU AND I. SO MY QUESTION IS THIS: HAVEN'T YOU EVER LIKED SOMEONE AND WANTED TO TELL THEM BUT WONDERED IF IT'S THE RIGHT (AS IN CORRECT) THING TO DO? SIGN TO ME SOMETIME OR FEIGN EDITORIAL CRISIS SO WE CAN TALK ABOUT THIS SUBJECT.

I gotta love Linus for his trim sentences, his forthrightness, his out-there-ness. Reading his message gives me nervous energy—a need to either rip up the note and forget I ever saw it, or call him right now and hear what he has to say immediately.

Neither of those things happens, though, because—

"Cyrie Bergerac? You can go to room four."

ℓ

"Rhinoplasty can alter the shape or size of the nose. Increase the tip or decrease. Narrow the nostrils' span…"

"The span of the nostrils," I say back to Dr. Schnoz who is sitting behind his oversized wooden desk and sifting through cards as he recites the nose-worthy verbiage to me. "Sounds like an unpublished poem."

He looks at me and smiles. "See? Right there—a reason not to do it." He shakes his head.

"I thought you would want people to get this done." I grin and wave my hand across my face. "This is your primary income, is it not?"

"Cyrie," he says, "I've known your dad since college. You since you were a kid. A baby."

I lean back in my chair, the way you're not supposed to for fear of tipping over. "Ah, the good old days. Back when it"—I touch the offending body part—"was just a little thing."

He rolls his eyes and places his hands on his desk. "All I'm saying—and no, your parents didn't put me up to this—is that with wit like yours, with brains—"

"Who needs a good face?" I've heard it before. I've thought it before. But it's not true. "The thing is, I don't *need* it. I *want* it. I know the difference." I exhale deeply and study the trim on his desk. "But thanks for the confidence boost."

Dr. Schnoz claps his hands to switch gears. "Okay." He fiddles with the mouse on his desk and presses a button so a screen rises from the floor. Instantly a photo of me appears, enlarged. "We can change whatever you want, of course. You can trim here…" He clicks and instantly reduces the length of my nose.

"It's jarring." I stare at the image ahead, amazed at my face.

"It is," he confirms. "We could change the angle between your nose and lip. Where you've been used to this…" He clicks again and suddenly I have a different nose. "You can play with the shape."

I'm glued to the screen, all the different versions of me appearing next to one another each time he clicks. A group of Cyries. Each one able to be just like me, but different. Short and perky nose. Elegant and long. Solid but not awkward. All of them are… "They're so normal."

"Yup. You pick it—just like apples."

I pick at my cuticles and point to one of the pictures. "That one's pretty nice. I choose that one."

"You sure?" He swivels in his seat to look at me with his pen poised.

I twist my mouth, unsure. "Probably. Maybe." Then I grin and stand up. The procedure, as he calls it—the "surgery" as my parents call it, to remind me how big a deal it is—is the simplest route to the solution. "Just out of curiosity: could you make it bigger?"

This makes him laugh. "You got it all, kiddo. Enjoy." He holds the door open for me. "We've scheduled you for mid-January? Correct?"

I nod. "Correct." A correction. That's what it is, really. A correction to a problem. A few more months and, just like one of those Cyries on the wall, I will be—if not picture-perfect— then at least photo-ready. And ready for more than that.

ℓ

That night, before I deal with homework and essays, I call Linus. Better to deal with this situation head-on. Or ear-on, as the phone would have it.

"Hey," I say, and he knows just who it is without my saying my name.

"So?"

"So..." I look at his note again. "I think..." How

should I say it without hurting his feelings? Without rejecting him outright? "I think you should make sure of how you really feel—"

"I know how I really feel, Cyrie." His voice is strong, confident.

"Oh, um…" I wasn't expecting ardency from him. "Then I guess…"

"Presumably you know how I'm feeling?" He waits for my response, and I know him well enough that I can tell his eyebrows must be raised in wonderment.

"I do." But I don't. I don't feel the same way. "You know what, Linus? Remember how when you start an op-ed piece, you're supposed to get attention but also get your point across right away?" He gives a grumble as I try and distract him to buy myself more time. I can't just come out and say I don't like him in that way, because he's too nice for that. I want him to get how I feel without my having to explain it.

"I feel like I'm going nuts, though. Or I will if I don't get this off my chest."

Not here. Not now, I think and hurry to quiet him up. "Save it. Seriously, the more passion gathers inside you, the better, right?" Not really, but I'm flustered and wishing the person on the other end of the phone line was Eddie.

"But I—"

"But then just tell me—I mean, tell your person how you feel at the best time possible, okay? Because it matters not just *how* you feel but *how you find out* about the other person's feelings." Possibly this is the most poorly constructed sentence ever uttered. Possibly if I write that way on my application, Sarah Jensen will have no competition for Harvard.

But Linus just says, "Okay. I think I get what you're saying."

"Good," I say. At least someone does, because I'm beginning to confuse even myself.

ℓ

When I check the Sumbodee account that night, I'm dismayed to find that Eddie's lengthy, personal email is going to be answered with this, from Leyla:

> *Hi Rox—*
>
> *I saw how fast you wrote back. You must be a really quick typer! I'm maybe only thirty words per minute but I'm faster when I have good music playing which I do right now (The Shins). Your not going to believe this, but I am almost done with college applications and I'm so happy about it. Do you know where your going? I heard maybe someplace in England—that would be so cool! I could visit you there and have tea with the queen.*

See ya later!

Leyla

I wish she translated onto the page better. Her queen comment could have been funny—with her silly voices and sweet demeanor—but here it reads vapid. That's the problem, I realize, as I correct the your/you're issues. She's not saying anything; she's just writing. I want so badly to do more than edit—to write about how the Shins' music is so emotive and even though you can't tell what the hell they're saying sometimes, you still respond. How Oxford would be incredible and how I went punting on the river there two summers ago and felt as though I existed in another era; how wistful and wonderful it made me feel. But I can't do that, because that's me. Not her. So I punctuate and press *send*.

twelve

erfect!" Leyla gives me a thumbs-up in drama class before she takes her seat. No doubt she is commenting on the flurry of emails I've proofed, cleaned up, and added to over the past few days. Her grammar has improved, though not the depths of her commentary. He knows, now, that she likes grilled cheese with tomato and never wears boots in the winter, and used to want to be a professional tap dancer. But not much else. He's brought up some issues, but kept the tone fairly chatty. I guess that's just how it goes. Meanwhile, my brain is yet again crammed with things I want to say to him, but can't.

I once told Leyla that I wished I was average. She couldn't understand why, even though she tried. She listened, but she wound up asking, "Why wouldn't you want to be, um, super-modely if you could?" I tucked nearly my whole face into my turtleneck and mumbled, "Plain. Plain would be enough."

I make it through Drama, barely keeping my eyes open during the monologues. My neck starts to ache from keeping my head up, and I use my clear view of Eddie and the idea of the approaching auction to keep my brain from switching off. Eddie's focused on underlining his lines, even though he doesn't have to perform until next week, when I have to, also. Memorizing comes pretty easily to me, and I have my words down, but I need to work on the delivery if I want to get a decent grade. Harold is nothing if not a stickler for at least attempting to perform properly.

"I really care about you," Jack Schneider monotones. His eyes are glued to his shoes, and his body is stiff.

I watch Eddie look at him and grin. Not meanly, just in his wry fashion. That's the great thing about Eddie—or one of them, anyway. He's funny and smart without being cruel. He coughs, which gets Jack to look up. Eddie sits up straight and uses his hands to gesture, some sports signal that must mean something I don't get, but suddenly Jack is giving an Oscar-worthy speech about truly loving someone and understanding their core, and it's enough to make my eyes well up. I look at Leyla, but she's basically asleep in her cushy chair—one of the hazards of having class in a darkened room.

ℓ

"That was so nice of you," I say to Eddie when we're out of the dark, in the stark light of science lab. Eddie doesn't answer. "Hello?" I wait for a few seconds and then poke him with one of the tongue depressors we're using to stir.

"What?" Sheepishly, he looks at me. "Sorry—I'm kind of out of it." His eyes focus on me, but then glaze over.

"With Jack Schneider?" I remind him. "He was tanking, and then…"

"Yeah," Eddie nods. "No big deal."

"I know, but still. You're very…" I pause, pretending to be absorbed in the chemical process in front of us. "Kind."

"At least you didn't say 'nice.' No guy wants to be called nice." He goes back to his cloud of non-focus, his hands on the cold soapstone lab table.

Nice. That's what I would have said to Linus if I'd thought it through, though maybe after Eddie's comments on the word I won't. The thing is, Linus *is* nice. And cute. And bright. But not for me. I scratch my nose and then hate that I did that—it'll be red now and announce itself even more than usual.

Without thinking, I start humming "Come Dancing" by the Kinks. The notes are out of my mouth for only a few seconds before I remember that Eddie and Leyla (by way of me) exchanged thoughts about that very band online last night. I quickly switch to the Alphabet Song to cover up, even though it makes a couple of girls snicker nearby. Eddie doesn't even notice.

"Tired or something?" I ask. My pulse speeds up at being so near him, but I remain calm. I think back to all the emails, the way he listens to—or hears, or reads—everything and comments on it like it matters. Or matters to him.

"Or something," he responds, his voice laced with mystery.

I jot down the amount of fluid added to the beaker. "Meaning?"

"Meaning…" He looks over his shoulder and all around to make sure no one's eavesdropping. "Your correspondence is…"

My correspondence? Cue racing pulse. How could he know? He couldn't. "I didn't write anything…" I spit out while stirring.

Eddie's hand flies up to wave me off. "No, no that's not what I mean—the email thing you set up is all I'm talking about." He waits, then catches my eye. "It's kind of great in some ways. Even better than I hoped. She's, like, this mixture of sweet and salty…"

I make a face. "Like kettle corn?"

He laughs. "That's like something *she'd* say." My hands start to shake as he stares at me. "I can tell you guys hang out a lot."

My hands stop shaking, but my heart pounds. "Oh."

"But…" Eddie takes out a pen. His eyes look sorry. "So,

anyway, thanks for everything. I look forward to my email. Probably too much."

"Why 'too much'?" I smile at him, thinking how, really, he's complimenting me. He's saying how much he likes *me*. My writing. But then my smile fades when I remember that he doesn't know this, that all of these words, the flurries of letters, amount to nothing—at least for me.

He frowns. "I'm thinking… maybe it's not a good idea anymore."

My heart slams inside my chest. "Why? I mean, why not?"

Eddie clears his throat and adjusts the temperature on our burner. "Because it's…" He thinks and looks right at me. "In some ways I feel closer to her, but in other ways, it's more…"

"Distancing?" I offer and wish I'd kept quiet. Eddie nods. I so don't want to stop writing to him; I don't want Leyla to stop writing. My initial wariness about being involved is so far gone, and I feel addicted to his words. "But you're only just getting started with this…"

He considers. "Maybe… maybe if you could just…" He shakes his head, but I encourage him with my eyes to go on. "Think you have it in you to get her to open up?"

"What do you mean? I've been—she's been so open, don't you think?"

Eddie shrugs. "I don't know. I get the feeling that she's holding back. That there's more to say but she's afraid."

"Maybe she *is* afraid." I think about the exhilaration

of holding his hand in the dark box, the fear that we could never do that in broad daylight, the worry that even online, rejection lies around the corner.

He lowers his voice to a near-whisper. "She's gotta let it out, you know? Otherwise, it's pointless. The fear stuff, the things she's afraid of, that's what I want to know. I can talk about liking grilled cheese with her anywhere."

Ah, the grilled cheese rears its greasy head. Getting Leyla to say more than that will be like pulling teeth. She's so uptight about the emails—not at all her relaxed, goofy, and approachable self. She's the only mean-crew girl (former or otherwise) who has ever been more than civil to me. If only she'd open up on the page. "I'll relay the message."

"Really?" Eddie grins his thanks and exhales with relief. "Anyway," he adds, jotting a few notes into our lab book, "I better write down the results of our experiment."

I catch up with Leyla at the *Word* office, where she and Linus and Nicole Marchese are working on layout. Nicole hunches over her papers, writing notes in all caps as she's always done, while Linus looks on. Leyla nimbly arranges icons, clicks articles into place, and formats the week's issue.

"That looks great!" I slop my bag onto a chair and lean over to read.

"We're about to finish up," Nicole says, her eyes weary. "I'm in need of strong coffee."

"Me, too. Even though I don't drink coffee. I was up a lot last night," Leyla says, her hands in constant motion, "wondering why this issue was so hard for us to do. I realized it's because we have so many little items."

"Plus the extended auction info," Linus adds. He sneaks a look at me as though wanting an answer I can't give, and I ignore it. "Leyla's got a knack for figuring out solutions, I think."

Leyla smiles. "Thanks. It's like . . . " She looks at us, animated and happy. "I can visualize all the stuff in my mind and slip the articles into place. Then I have to just match the image in my mind with the screen. And . . . viola!"

I look at her. "*Voilà*, remember?"

Linus laughs. "Leyla, you crack me up."

She blushes but shrugs, not embarrassed the way she might be if Eddie were around or the Von Schmedler pack, where she tries to keep a low profile so as not to compete with Wendy. "I'm not a wordsmith like this one here." She thumbs at me. "But I got it going on with the layout. Guess I'm bound for map-making school or something."

I sit down and listen to their easy banter, trying to avoid even casual contact with Linus—no editorial hand on the shoulder, no arms touching on the messy table.

When Linus excuses himself to get snacks for everyone, I use the two minutes to talk to Leyla.

"More?" she asks. "He wants more?" Her voice is incredulous, her face wide-eyed with dismay. "I'm sick of having to worry about what to say. No way can I give him more. It's all I can do to think of topics at all."

I wrinkle my mouth. "That's not true. You have lots to say—think about how you were just talking in here. Let the words just spill out." I swallow my pride and feelings and shove any traces of love for Eddie down to my toes. "He wants to know all the stuff you don't tell anyone. The things that keep you up at night."

Leyla's slender shoulders slump in her thin, berry-colored cashmere sweater. "I'm not sure I can do that, Cyrie. How're you supposed to tell someone else those things when you don't even like to admit they're there?"

All I can do is nod, because... "You're totally right. But I think..." Linus comes back and I hurry up. "Just try a little more, because you don't want him to stop writing, do you?" I watch her response—it's somewhere between a no and a shrug. My own response is much more clear. "You don't. Trust me."

She nods just as Linus hands her a cheese stick. She accepts it and says, "Thanks. Did you know that I used to live in Wisconsin? Every time I have these things I feel like I'm back in cheese country."

Linus eats a cracker and looks amused. "You learn something new every day." Then he winks at me.

e

The days fly by in a haze of more emails—lines from them stick with me:

Would you rather eat one chocolate-covered beetle or a pile of ants?

... I'm not sure I believe in God necessarily, but I believe in something...

... I used to wish I lived by the beach so I could wake up everyday and be in the sand and by the water but now I'm glad I don't because it makes summer that much better...

So are you saying you can't be with the thing you love all the time because it gets stale?

No, not at all. More like I appreciate it more because I'm not growing immune to it every day.

I'm the opposite. I enjoy things—beaches, people, songs— even more when I'm around them a lot. When I know them.

You're pretty incredible, you know that?

You know that? Do I know that? I do know that, even if I know it about someone else. And I've managed to retain enough brain power through all the writing to recall that all of his words, his beautiful, thoughtful words, are not really meant for me. They're meant for—

"Leyla! Hi!" I wave to her by the rows of lockers and she saunters over in her new jeans and bright orange sweater. (I'd never wear a color so bright—not just because I look ill in them but because I feel more comfortable, less noticeable, in darker colors.) I wouldn't say Leyla's guilty of plagiarizing my thoughts, because all I really did was make the words flow a bit more smoothly, doused the letters with a bit of humor to break up the getting-to-know-you stuff, to keep Eddie interested. Added a little bit of my mental musings. And the emails are saved in the account so she can read them—and so far, Leyla hasn't protested my additional verbs, nouns, and adjectives.

"Could I be any more leafy in my sweater?" She plucks at the wool. "Not green leaf, but … "

"Autumnal. Yeah. You look nice." I smile at her and ignore the stares from a few underclassmen who walk by and point at me.

"You all set for tonight? Here." She hands me a piece of paper shaped like a pumpkin.

I study the triangle eyes, the jagged mouth. "I can't believe she makes you actually bring the invite." In an attempt to be even more elitist and annoying, Wendy asks her waxy, accessorized mom to print up invitations to her infamous get-togethers, including tonight's Halloween festivities, lest the underlings and wannabees show up.

"Well, believe me, if you don't have a pumpkin, you can't get in." Leyla's smile freezes; down at the other end of the corridor, Eddie is tacking a poster for the auction on the wall.

"A little to the left!" I yell at him. His smile is visible from quite a distance and he gives me a thumbs-up in the most sarcastic way possible. I adore him.

Leyla swallows hard and breathes as though she, too, has a jagged mouth. I pocket the pumpkin. "What's wrong?" I slam my locker shut.

"Nothing. Everything." She pauses. "We've had so many emails."

I give her a hard look. "Um, I know that. I'm the one sending them, remember?" *And writing them*, I think but don't say. Either Leyla's not reading them too closely, or she's too caught up to notice my slight add-ons and retouches. Then again, I'm the editor. She's used to being staff and just working on the project at hand.

"Well, it's now or never," Leyla says. I wait for her to say more. Eddie holds the masking tape in his mouth and I think back to our last email—how he defined his favorite dessert as being lemon meringue pie the color of melted butter. How it was so clear I could taste it. How now that we're writing more, the details mean everything.

"He's going on his college tour starting Sunday," Leyla finally says. She clutches her books to her chest. "So I'm going to kiss him tonight."

The sweet taste of imagined desserts fades instantaneously, replaced with only lemon. Something bitter.

thirteen

I'm going out!" I shout, hoping my parents can hear me from their room, where they're tucked away nursing colds and watching black-and-white movies.

My dad's head appears at the top of the stairs. "I thought it was Halloween?"

"Last time I checked, yeah." I shuffle the candy around in the bowl, searching for malted milkballs. Finding none, I put the bowl back by the door. "Are you sure you don't want me to stay home and deal with the trick-or-treaters?" Our street is heavily trafficked by little ghosts, goblins, the latest fad costumes, and a pod of parents making sure all goes well. Later, the slightly-too-old-to-be-doing-this crowd comes out to clean up the remaining sweets and pester those whose porch lights are switched off.

"We're fine," my mom yells down, but her nose is stuffed up so it sounds like "beer twine."

"Good name for a band, beer twine." I smirk. "I won't be late."

"But, Cyrie?" Dad's face is flushed, his voice scratchy. "You're not dressed."

I survey my attire. "Unless jeans, boots, and a clean black turtleneck sweater count as not dressed, then I'm confused."

"Boo yuk mice."

"Thanks, Mom."

"You should have a costume," Dad insists.

I sigh. "Every day's a costume, what can I say?" My parents don't try to make me feel differently. They know better by now. I grab a Kit Kat (not even on my second tier of favorite candies) and head out the door.

By the time I park my parent's car with the herd of others at the end of Wendy's long driveway, the party is in full swing. Couples are entwined on car fronts, a few guys are playing glow-in-the-dark Frisbee, and a plethora of vixens in sultry outfits parade the grounds. I should have dressed up—but in what?

"Hey—finally!" Leyla's the world's most adorable ghost. "I

couldn't find anything else, so I went with simple and elegant." She twirls so I can admire her white sheet as we head inside.

"I feel dumb in normal clothes," I say, stepping onto the oversized floor mat that reads *Welcome* in such heavy, bold letters that it makes me feel anything but.

"Nice mask!" Beef spews at me as he sips a beer and laughs.

"She's not wearing a mask!" Leyla defends me before realizing she's made it worse.

Beef laughs again, and begins to rehash his Night of Knights jousting using the fireplace tools in Wendy's living room.

"Well, this is a recipe for disaster," I say, pointing to the sharp objects, but also meaning my face on this night of costumes and creepiness. "Did I ever tell you how much I loathe Halloween?"

"Why?" Eddie saunters up and hands one caramel-covered apple to me and one to Leyla. He's dressed in a ruffled shirt and tights, recycled from Night of Knights, but enhanced with a quill pen and a scroll made from a paper-towel roll. "Get it?" he gestures with the quill. "I'm the Bard. As in Shakespeare."

"Toil and trouble," I say, feeling my whole body respond to him. I want to hug him and laugh with him and sit on the roof of a car and watch the parade of costumes in the moonlight with him.

He stares at Leyla. "Aren't you going to try the apple?"

"Are we getting biblical now?" I ask and try to laugh. Then I think about Leyla's decree—that tonight's the night their lips will meet—and feel sick.

Leyla shakes her head. "I'm not ... I don't really like ... " She pauses, as if she has to gather her strength to say the word. "Apples."

Eddie looks confused. "But I thought you said ... "

I kick Leyla. "You do. You do like apples. A lot." She pulls the billowing sheet closer to her and flinches. When she elbows me back, and I can see the edges of the sheet start to shake from her wobbling legs.

"I do?" She looks at me. "Oh, I do. Only ... "

"Only ... " I fill in for her. "Only I didn't have dinner so I'll have both apples." I grab hers and begin to eat it and my own with more gusto than I should, because with the sticks and the shape of my nose, I can't actually get my mouth on the fruit without tipping my face awkwardly to the side or approaching the bite from above like a plane trying to land on a too-small airstrip. They both watch, horrified.

"Do you need ... ?" Eddie starts.

Leyla wrinkles her face. "Do you want to cut it?"

At first I think she means my nose—to which the answer is yes—and then I see she means the apple. I nod, so she goes off to retrieve a knife from Wendy's enormous kitchen.

Wendy chooses this moment—my time of glory—to emerge from the shadows and cast her glare on me.

"No costume needed, I see?"

"Well, if it isn't the wasted witch of the west," I say as she totters up. Caramel sticks to my teeth and apple juice drips onto my chin, but I do my best to keep it together.

"Show me your invite or get out."

I plead with Eddie to reach into my back pocket and get the dumb pumpkin paper. He does, and I feel his fingers on my back. Shivers prick my skin and I could fall into a swoon if it weren't for the mess on my face and the company of witches. "Satisfied?"

Wendy laughs at the slop on my sweater, the stick in my hair, and nods. "Absolutely!" She leaves.

I head off to the bathroom to clean up, disrupted once in mid-pee by an elf who has over-imbibed and then by Leyla, who has borrowed a pumpkin costume that barely fits through the doorway. She pushes her padded orange self through and looks at me with teary eyes.

"I spilled fake-blood punch on my sheet," she moans.

I shrug. "It's not that big a deal. You're a decent jack-o'-lantern."

Leyla shakes her head, sad, and the stem of her pumpkin-top hat wilts. "I can't do it." She wipes her dripping mascara with a tissue, then adds, "Sorry to invade your privacy, by the way. But we're close enough to pee in front of each other, right?" She takes off the hat and puts her head in her hands.

"I've never seen such a sad squash." I pull my pants up and wash my hands.

"I'm not a squash!" she yells with more force than necessary. "I'm a pumpkin. You know that." I look at her as if to suggest, yeah, and... "Oh—a pumpkin is a squash. God, I am the dumbest creature on the planet."

Hearing her say this makes my eyes well up. "You're not! Don't say that—Leyla! You are not dumb."

"It was going well until... he said something about the stars of Orion and I asked who Ryan was."

I laugh. "You're funny! See?"

"No, really." Leyla's hair is matted, her cheeks streaked. "Who's Ryan?"

"*Orion*." I adjust my shirt and wonder why I'm the only person at the party without a costume, except for a girl named Virginia Clapham who dresses in all black every day and doesn't wear costumes for "political reasons." "Orion, the constellation?"

"I thought he was like, 'Oh, Ryan.' Then it got worse—he says stuff I don't get and I'm standing there and he asks my opinion about locally harvested food and I'm....." She looks at me in the mirror. "I thought he was going to kiss me. I really did." Then she begins to bawl. "It's so hard to be with him. I just want it to be... like putting on your favorite sweater."

I stare at her. "*That*. Right there. That was poetry, Leyla." She doesn't believe me, so I go on. "So you mix up words.

So you don't always lead the pack when it comes to figuring things out." I pat her on the back of her felt-padded costume and look at our reflections in the mirror. "You always know what to do when someone feels down. You give amazingly thoughtful gifts. You make funny faces—and hey, I'm the queen of the funny face. And ... and you rock with layout."

She sighs, reeling in her emotions. "But I can't talk to him. Not face-to-face, anyway."

Right then, I make a decision. "Come with me," I tell her. "And get rid of the squash suit. Grab us two sheets and a pair of scissors."

We hide out in Wendy's cavernous upstairs bathroom amidst a startling array of every potion, lotion, cream, and makeup known to mankind.

"Think she's got enough here?" I ask, holding up a bottle labeled *Firming Serum*. "Here's one called 'Sweetness.' Dream on, Wendy."

Leyla takes it from me and pools the sheets by her feet. "She has this? You wouldn't believe how much two ounces of this stuff costs. 'Sweetness' has a waiting list a mile long." She shakes her head and puts it back. "Must be a gift from her mom."

I stick out my tongue. "I wouldn't know whether to be thankful or hurt if my mom got me cover-up or something."

Leyla pauses, thoughtful, before she slides the scissors into the matching floral sheets (swiped from the back of the massive linen closet) and cuts out eyeholes. "Maybe Wendy doesn't, either."

We try on our matching outfits. In the mirror, now, we're no longer at opposite ends of the spectrum of teenage looks—we're not beauty and the beast. We're just girls in sheets. Two ghosts heading downstairs to get what we came for—a kiss.

"Call him over!" I tell her. Leyla and I try not to giggle as we hatch our scheme out by the thickly landscaped back garden. The air is crisp, verging on cold, and when Leyla shouts for Eddie, I can think of nothing better than warming myself in his arms.

"Now, go for it." I duck into the prickly topiary. Leyla stands with her arms inside the sheet, motionless.

"Hey." Eddie has his sword out, but uses it like a cane as he approaches. "Thought you'd gone."

"Um, nope." Leyla's voice quavers. "I'm here. Right here."

"Good."

They stand there without saying much, their silence highlighted by the nearby noise from the party. Whoops, shouts, and laughter only make the awkwardness between them more evident.

I cough to stir things along, and then hope Eddie didn't hear me.

Leyla acts like I've kicked her into gear. "So…do you like pirate movies or anything like that?"

From between the thickly set branches, I can just make out Eddie's face. He looks half-confused and half sad. "They're okay. Not in my top ten." He shrugs.

"What is your top ten?" Leyla asks.

I breathe a sigh of relief—at least now they're talking.

"Movies? Well, you gotta have the whole *Fletch*, *Groundhog Day*, *Caddyshack* thing in there." He waits for more from Leyla, then goes on. "And then, just so I don't appear totally humor-obsessed… *The Philadelphia Story*."

"I went to Philadelphia once," Leyla offers. "I had cheesesteak. They're famous for that."

"I know." Eddie's got his bored-out-of-his-mind voice on, the same one he uses when the *Word* meetings go too long, the same one I'd follow with, "Story at eleven."

Eddie clears his throat and tries again. "After our emails, you know, I was kind of hoping…" he touches her sheeted shoulder. "Flannel."

"Yeah, it's soft." Leyla laughs, her voice filled with nerves. I hope she doesn't throw up; then again, if she does, at least she can use the sheet for cleaning purposes.

"Tell me what it is about me that makes you want to write all that stuff to me." He peers into her circle-eyes. She says nothing, but her legs shake—I can see it even under the sheet. "Name one thing that stands out for you. About me."

Leyla's feet scrape the flagstone path as she takes a step backwards. "You're..."

Inquisitive, I think. "You're..." *Able to see the best in people even when they don't deserve it.* "You're..." Before I can fill in another blank, Leyla says, "Hot."

Eddie's face demonstrates his surprise. "Hot?" He crosses his arms.

Leyla reassures him, as though he doubts her. "No, really, you're very hot. Boiling. And you're a total jock, which is great, right? I mean, you work out, and...and..."

He stares at her and shakes his head. "Why are you doing this?" He looks down at his shoes like he wants them to explain. Then he looks back at her. "Maybe this—" he points to her sheet, and to his ruffled shirt "—isn't the best idea after all."

Slowly, he starts back up the stone stairs toward the house, toward the sounds of people actually having a good time. Leyla turns to me. She moves her hands out from under the sheet, holds them out, asking me *now what?*

I think fast. Immediate action must be taken lest this whole thing implode. And then I'll be left to deal with the fallout from all fronts. I wave her over, and she crouches down in the bushes with me.

"Yell to him," I tell her.

"Eddie! Come back!" Leyla's voice gets him to stop. "Great," she whispers to me. "Now he's just standing there. What the hell am I supposed to do?"

"I'm thinking."

"Well, think quicker."

"What for?" Eddie shouts. "Because I'm such a hottie?" He slings the line as part humor, but the dismay in his voice floats all the way down to our hiding spot.

"Tell him you were just nervous," I command her, buying time.

Leyla slides the sheet off and cups her hands, muffling her voice slightly as she shouts. "I was just scared, you know. Nervous. I'm not good under ... "

"Under spontaneous circumstances," I fill in.

"What?" she whispers.

"Under spontaneous circumstances!"

"Spontaneous!" she shouts. "I can't do spontaneous!"

Eddie gives a quiet laugh. "Oh, yeah? What can you do?"

Leyla looks like she might throw up on me. She covers her mouth with her hand and pleads with me with her eyes. "I can quote lyrics like you wouldn't believe," I say, changing the pitch of my voice just a little.

"You sound funny," Eddie says, taking a step back toward us.

"Just stay there!" I yell, and nearly pop out of the bush to make him stand far enough away that we're hidden. "I don't want ... I'm less nervous from here."

Eddie pushes his hands through his hair and sits on the steps. "Well, fine. For now, I guess. So, then, tell me what you really think about me. Am I just some guy you want to ask you to the prom, or what?"

Just the mention of the prom brings out my own wriggling worries and my hope that he'd ask me one day. Leyla opens her mouth, but I speak. "I don't even care about the prom that much..." I start. "Except maybe I do a little. The point is—you're not just hot. That's secondary. Or tertiary..."

"Tertiary?"

"I don't know that word! Don't make me sound better than I really am!" Leyla hisses, swatting my shoulder.

"Thirdy-dary, I mean. Secondary and thirdary—anyway, I think the best thing is that you always know what people need. Like in drama with Jack Schneider, how you kind of rescue everyone."

Eddie absorbs this. "Thanks."

I go on. "And you... when you look at me I can tell that there's so much happening in your mind. Like you want to pour everything onto the table for me to see, just so I can know all about you."

Leyla nudges me and whispers, "That was good." She peeks through the bushes. "He looks happy!"

"I do want you to know about me," Eddie is saying. "And just so you don't think I'm conceited or anything, it's not just about what you think of me." He clears his throat, his voice softer. "I think about your good qualities. And I want to be able to just talk. A lot. Not just talk, but..."

"And your writing. When I read it, I feel like I'm the most privileged person in existence."

Eddie stands up, moved enough to take a step closer. "I'm the privileged one. Everyone thinks they know you, but they don't. Not the way I do."

Leyla clutches my arm and then her heart. "I'm so loving this. Tell him how I really feel. Now."

I look at Leyla and watch her eyes, how they gleam with excitement, how her whole self seems poised to fall. "I could love you," I say, blurting it out before I can reel it back in.

Leyla pinches my sheet. "Ouch!" I squeal.

"That was too much," she says in angry whisper. "I semi-like the guy, but come on, 'love'?"

"What's going on down there?" Eddie asks.

I cover my tracks. "Oh, nothing! I'm just talking to myself—ouch. You know, like love can hurt. Or crushes can, anyway."

"You don't have to feel hurt," Eddie says, his voice soothing. "Come out of the forest and come over here."

"No!" Leyla and I say precisely at the same moment.

"Why not?" Eddie's voice grows louder. He leans to one side, trying to see exactly where the voice is coming from.

"Because you haven't said what you like about me," I say to him.

"That's easy," Eddie replies. "Your potential. You have basically everything anyone could ever want in another human being—sweetness, compassion, thoughtfulness. You're funny. You're athletic. You like cool music."

I eat it all up. Each and every word makes the cells in my body jump around. I lean forward, inching my way out of the bushes just slightly. "And?"

"And . . . I wouldn't be honest if I didn't say you were just about the most beautiful thing I've ever seen."

This comment sends me reeling—once when I think it's truly meant for me, and again when I realize it's not. Of course it's not.

Leyla has freed herself from the bushes, brushed off the remaining twigs, and made her way over to Eddie.

Wordlessly, he puts his arms around her waist and pulls her to him. Their faces are inches apart, bright in the new moonlight.

"Where's your costume?" he asks.

"Back there," Leyla points in my direction, where her sheet is puddled on the ground. I duck, even though I know they can't see me.

"Leave it behind for good," Eddie says. Without waiting for her response, he tucks his hands behind her head and puts his mouth on hers. They kiss for what seems like an eternity, connecting in the fall air, until Eddie leads her back toward the house.

And I am there, just a ghost, alone.

fourteen

*D*id you want some cream with your nose?" The new server at Any Time Now asks, his eyes pinned on my face.

"This is not a vestige from Halloween," I inform him, my voice pointed. "This is, in fact, real. Which is more than I can say for your efforts in the serving realm. Ever hear of a knife? Am I supposed to spread my butter with a fork?"

He looks at me as though the last thing in the world he wants to bring me is a knife. "Sorry. Sorry." He blushes and runs to the kitchen.

The café is decked out in an ode to the 1980s—graffiti on one wall, day-glo colors abounding, triangular tables with bubblegum-colored stools everywhere, Wham! on the sound system, and minuscule, highly stylized food arranged on giant plates. I eat my hexagonal mini-brownie and turn my attention back to my work.

"Hi!" Linus' voice saves me from the blankness that is my essay. "Nice to see you."

"Nice?" I'm not in the mood for Linus' positivity. He's always chipper. Always okay.

"I didn't mean anything by it," he says, grabbing a turquoise stool to sit on.

"Nice life," I say, remembering my lonely arrival home last night after Wendy's party. "Nice nose."

Linus gives me the sign for *enough*. "I heard what the guy said. He didn't mean anything by it."

"Yes," I say, looking at the server as he refills salt and pepper shakers with Hanna. Hanna's dressed in a power suit with giant shoulder pads, deeply tanned pantyhose with anklets over them, and high heels. Her eyes are rimmed in electric blue liner, and her hair is as large as a toaster and just as stiff. "He did. He meant to be mean. People think they're so subtle, but they're not."

Linus shakes his head, disapproving. "And what do you do? Be mean back?"

"God, don't get all supercilious on me." I chew on my pen cap. But this makes me think of Eddie and how he always has teeth marks on his ballpoints, so I stop.

Linus stands up. "What's wrong with you these days, Cyrie?" He studies me. "Where *are* you? I thought it was just college pressure or something, but you're not ... "

"I'm not the person you want me to be?" I ask, thinking about his note that we never talked about.

He waves that off. "No. I don't want you to be any particular way. Except, maybe, the nice person you could be if you'd only stop defending yourself, for once."

I meet his gaze. "What right do you have to tell me to stop defending myself? If I don't do it, who will?"

Linus' normally upbeat persona fades. His mouth is sad. "I don't know, Cyrie. I don't know anymore."

He leaves without telling me why he came in the first place, and I sit with my tiny food wishing I could fix everything. That I could clear my head enough to unclutter and simplify my life.

"Last night should have been ideal," I say to Hanna when it's closing time and I've scared away yet another server. "Trying on someone else's face? It's better than the noses at Dr. Schnoz's office."

"You're not still doing that ... procedure, are you?"

I flick my nose. "January 18th. I'm there. In the chair. Or, um, on the table or whatever." I flash forward to that day, to the relief I'll feel. "But last night? I couldn't wear a costume—you know why?" Hanna shakes her head. "Because I live in one. And no one can see me any differently."

Hanna wipes the counter and fixes one of her ridiculously long press-on nails. "No offense, Cyrie, but I think you're full of shit." She delivers this line as well as any of the ones from her cancelled television show.

I give her a steely glare. "How so?"

She tidies up while she talks, tucking cutlery away, folding napkins into stacks. "This is real life. You have the face you have, okay? So maybe you didn't turn out like that image you have of yourself—I sure as hell didn't think I'd be listening to 'Wake Me Up Before You Go Go' at my age and sweeping floors. I mean, I was on TV for God's sake!" She laughs and leans onto the counter. "But you know what? Deal with it. The reason you didn't wear a costume last night has nothing to do with how other people see you. You could've shown up as a cheetah, or a flapper in a wickedly cool dress and pearls, or a disco queen. But you went as you because you can't let go of yourself long enough to let anyone else in."

She continues her closing-up mission, leaving me to ruminate and wonder if maybe—maybe—she's a little bit right.

At school on Monday, I sneeze through History, Calculus, and French. By the time I get to lunch, I can hardly take the tissues away from my nose before having to—

"Look out folks, she's gonna blow!" Wendy pretends to duck for cover in the hallway. She faux-cowers and then gives a snorty laugh to Jill and their girl group.

Fever creeps into my cheeks, and I can feel a cough starting in my chest. I need to go home and crawl into bed, but I don't want to miss Drama and seeing Eddie. See him post–lip lock with Leyla.

"All the 'Sweetness' in the world couldn't cover up your flaws, huh, Wendy?" It's not one of my better put-downs, but Wendy looks like I've slapped her hard on the cheek. She blushes and walks away without another word.

I leave the cafeteria and find that Leyla's saved a seat for me in Drama. "Hey, you!" She goes to hug me but I stop her.

"I'm germ central right now."

She backs up. "Oh. Well, maybe this will make you feel better." She leans in and whispers. "Halloween was awesome! We kissed … "

"I know. I was right there, in the bushes?"

Leyla checks for spies and shushes me. "Right, but I mean, after that, we made s'mores with Wendy and everyone by the fireplace inside and sat together and—this is the cutest—he fed me the marshmallows!" She smiles, her eyes aglow. "Sorry

I was so incommunicatory over the weekend. My dad snagged the phone."

Incommunicado, I want to correct her, but I don't because I'm too caught up in the image of Eddie's fingers feeding Leyla mini-marshmallows. Maybe they weren't mini. Maybe they were big. Or shaped like pumpkins.

It's so sweet I want to throw up. But I don't, because this is just proof I shouldn't waste my efforts. "You look happy," I tell her. And she does. Her hair is bouncy, her smile wide, her body calm instead of jittery.

"We kissed again—he's just the best—"

"I get it. He's a good kisser." My heart feels upended. I look around. "So where is he?"

Leyla shrugs. "College tours, remember? He's gone all week." She sighs.

"What, you miss him already?" I wipe my nose. It's already raw underneath, and I wince each time I have to blot it.

"No, actually." She looks at her notebook and fiddles with her pen. Today it's a poppy, bright red and cheery—unlike her face all of a sudden. "The thing is, I'm kind of relieved."

I blow again. "What do you mean?" Harold comes in and gathers props for what is sure to be an interesting class.

"We're not writing this week. No emails, I mean. Phew!" She swipes her brow in dramatic fashion. "But seriously. I mean, after I got home, I felt all..." She mimes goose bumps on her arms. "But then, I thought back, and sometimes it's like we're not—" she looks at me "—on the same page. I'm not trying to be funny."

"But you kissed!" I say this as though she's crazy to feel anything other than thrilled.

"So what? Yeah, it was awesome, and yeah, he's super hot, and…but it feels weird to know you're with someone who wants so much from you." She twists her pen around and loops it into her hair so it forms a bun. "Sometimes I don't want that much from a guy. I just want to hang out. To be together and like each other without all that…"

"Probing?" I throw in.

"Makes me think of some outer space show, but yeah." She pauses, considering. "You like that kind of stuff. Maybe it's one reason we're good together as friends. I like to be, and you like to be, c, d, e, f, and so on." She cracks up. Her prettiness takes a back seat to her ease. "Don't you ever like to just not think? To have a clear mind?"

My chin drops to my chest. I nod. The sickness and her words swirl around me and I stand up. "I get what you're saying," I tell her. "And it'll be good for you to relax. I, on the other hand, need to go home."

"You okay?"

"Just sick," I say. "Sick and tired." I tell Harold I'm leaving, then blow my nose.

"Here." Leyla hands me her emergency packet of Kleenex.

"Thanks," I say.

"You look terrible." Concern fills her words. "Wait, not like..."

I take a breath, thinking of Linus, thinking of my cluttered head, thinking of all the stuff I spew out but how little I say. "I'm sure I do, Leyla." I hand her my *Word* notebook. "If I'm not back tomorrow, think you and Linus can handle some of the auction stuff? We need to check on sponsors, get ads placed for the programs, double-check the flowers and other things that are being delivered to the—"

"To Wilson Farms, I know. Weekend after Thanksgiving. I got it."

"And make sure the seating works—you know, not too crowded, but crowded enough that people get nervous and bid higher. And the paper! The regular issues... I know it's a lot, but... and anywhere you can insert the theme... " I look at her. "The—"

"Cornucopia," she says, proving something. "I remember the name, Cyr." She smiles at me, and I sniff and smile back. Leyla is still completely calm. "No problem. We'll get it covered."

fifteen

On my desk is a picture of me from last year, playing tennis. As a rule, I'm not one to pay homage to myself on film, but I like the shot because I didn't know my photo was being taken. Maybe I'm better caught off guard, when I don't have a chance to plan, edit, and worry—about how I look, about which angle will downplay the center of my face.

I'm staring at the picture when my dad knocks on my door. "Enter," I grunt, and he pokes his head in.

"Food for the sicky. Day three of the fall illness. Still not sleeping?" I shake my head *no*. "You sure you don't need to go to the doctor?" He slides a lunch tray of grilled cheese, tomato soup, and a brownie onto the desk.

"You know she'll say it's just a virus. Senioritis. Trying to avoid all that lies before me."

He picks up the picture. In it, I'm in full Westie gear, my legs poised, my racket back, about to deliver my signature cutting forehand. "You were great in that match."

I clear off wadded-up tissues so my lunch tray can fit in front of me, and study the picture. "We were playing Guilford. The best."

"Until you came and knocked them from their throne." Dad uses a booming voice.

I cover my ears. "Ow. Headache. But yeah, we crushed them." I sigh and pick at the crust of my sandwich. The girl I'd played against took the defeat well, shaking my hand and saying how well I played. Then she saw my nose, let out a guffaw, and trotted back to her teammates feeling like she hadn't lost that badly.

"You crushed them—single-handedly, I believe."

"I probably could have done better."

"But you won, Cyrie." Dad takes a corner of the brownie for himself. "Why bother editing what you can't change?"

I'm about to nod and half-heartedly relive my varsity days, but I frown instead. "I wish everything were as easy as that. As thwacking the ball or scoring a point or devising a plan to win."

Dad puts his wide hands on my shoulders and kisses the

top of my head. "Wouldn't that be boring?" I shrug. "Maybe winning isn't as important as—"

"Don't say 'playing the game.' Cliché, man."

"Playing the game." He laughs.

"Besides," I add, "I'm a good editor."

"Let me know if you need anything." He steps out the door and then pokes his head back in. "Just remember that old saying about editors."

I stick my nose into a wad of tissues and retreat to my bed. "What's that?"

"Good editors edit. Great editors stop."

After he leaves, I look out the window at the autumnal scene. Everything is movie-perfect. Bright mums burst with orange and deep reds, pumpkins cluster on my neighbors' doorsteps. If only more yellow leaves would fall, then the ground would be evenly coated.

"Jeez—I'm editing nature now!" I say aloud, putting my head into my hands.

I try again to sleep off my viral germs but then reach for my laptop instead, pulling the hard shell of it onto my bed, half under the covers. With Linus and Leyla covering paper duties and my homework pretty much done (save for my college essay), there's not much to do. So I clean out and organize my email in-box, creating files for emails I want to keep and discarding hundreds of others.

I lie back on my pillows. What I want to do is talk to

Eddie. He'd make some crack about my voice being nasal, and I wouldn't even mind because he'd say it in a gentle way.

I look out the window one more time, as though a ghost might be watching me. Feeling the familiar pangs, I log on to the Sumbodee account.

"Just rereading," I mutter, and indulge myself with the rest of my lunch and Eddie's words. I go back to the beginning and read every note from him, savoring his phrases and pairing them in my mind with his physical self. Even though he's miles away looking at colleges right now, the letters make me feel closer to him. I'm about to do my sigh-and-pack-it-up routine when I refresh the page, and find a new email.

I bite my lip. It's not for me. Not really. Well, it kind of is. Then I shake my head. It wasn't my lips that got kissed last Friday. My body stayed cloaked in the ghost sheet while Leyla's . . . I click and read.

> *Question:*
>
> *How hard is it to focus on interview questions when all I want to do is be with you?*
>
> *Answer:*
>
> *Very.*

My heart flutters, even though I know he means her. Not me. But still. In my feverish state, my overly edited state, I pause: I want to write back. But I can't. Or I shouldn't. But another email pops through.

> *Okay, so I know we aren't supposed to write*
> *while I'm gone, but now I'm feeling like that*
> *was a dumb rule. Why shouldn't we just*
> *keep talking (or typing)? That way when*
> *I'm back we'll have even more to say.*

I could do nothing. I could call Leyla and tell her to write back—but then she'd know I was in the account for no reason...no reason except frothing over Eddie. But I want him to write more—to talk to me—and to have him hear me, too.

With the wind-swirled leaves outside and my feet warm under the blankets, I do what I should have done long ago. What I need to do. I stop editing and just write.

> *I'm so glad to hear from you! A week is way*
> *too long to go without the usual barrage of*
> *notes back and forth.*

I send it, and it isn't until I reread it that I notice the word "barrage" and wonder if that will give him pause—it's not really a Leyla word. But he writes back.

> *I'm sitting here in the library at Dartmouth*
> *wondering where I'll spend the next four*

years of my life. Where should I go to school?
What should I do with my life? Even though
I'm the one being judged here (or, um, inter-
viewed), I don't feel particularly qualified to
make these decisions.

I turn onto my stomach and type, burrowing my feet further under the sheets.

Maybe we're not qualified, and we should have
some other system set up so that someone other
than us (and the colleges) can make the choice
for us. An independent committee of sorts.

I type on and on, then send and wait for a response. It's better than IMs because we're writing more, saying full thoughts with no abbreviations—emotional or otherwise. We get to the point where we're overlapping, him sending, me sending—and saying everything.

When I was seven I thought I was cool because
I was old enough to have a bubble bath while
my parents were doing breathing exercises (yes,
true) downstairs. I always thought their deep-
breaths-in, deep-breaths-out were lame (verg-
ing on weird), so I went upstairs and ran the
bath, added an appropriate amount of lav-

ender-scented bubble bath, and went to get a book from my bedroom to read while soaking. But! I got the book and began reading, then forgot about the bath, forgot I'd put the water on full, and it wasn't until my dad yelled "Oh, shit!" or something like that (which is very unusual for him) that I looked up from the page. Turns out, water had filled not only the bathroom but the hallway. It seeped into the cracks and found its way into the kitchen via the ceiling, and dripped onto my parents, giving them the antithesis of relaxation.

Eddie writes back:

That's a lot of water. But I sense you're not talking about water.

I answer him, my cheeks flushed, my fingers moving quickly on the keyboard.

No. I'm using this charming story to get across my point that
a) I don't take baths anymore
b) I get absorbed in certain activities and tend to forget the rest of the world
c) Everything that I have inside I'm pouring

out to you right now like I've had it bottled
up forever

I wait for his response, wondering how many seconds will go
by before I hear the in-box ping.

> *I'm going to say b and c and leave the bath*
> *question open for further (ahem!) discussion.*
> *And if you're wondering whether I'm feeling*
> *the same way, the answer is yes. I'm hundreds*
> *of miles away (and will be more than one*
> *thousand miles away tomorrow, when I go to*
> *Michigan), but I feel like I'm sitting next to*
> *you and we're more than talking fast. It's like*
> *we're able to trade brains for a second (even*
> *though that's a really bizarre image). More*
> *than varsity, more than goals or the golden*
> *Westie award, or the paper, or anything, I've*
> *wanted to find (and I'm cringing while I*
> *write this but then again, I'm hundreds of*
> *miles away!) a best friend. And more than*
> *a friend. And I'm thinking that I've found*
> *both. HOWEVER, I might be way off base.*

Outside, the sky shifts from day to night. My lunch is long
gone cold, and my heart is filled. I carefully type back.

> *You are not off base. You are home.*

sixteen

For the next few days, the germs continue to march through my body, giving me symptoms that alternate from queasiness to stuffiness, shivers to sweats—but the whole time, I am more than happy.

"For a kid who's home from school, you are suspiciously chirpy," my mother says, eyeing me as I trudge from my room to the bathroom to slather some cream on my chapped nose.

"I'm sick," I say with the nasal voice to prove it. "I'm just…"

She studies my face and, motherly, tucks a strand of hair behind my ear, her hands fluttering around my cheeks. "You're—"

I watch her eyes. They're green like mine, and carry in them worlds of words. "I'm fine," I assure her, reaching for the cream. In the mirror I look miserable. My face does not accurately convey the bursting feelings I have inside, from late nights typing through various time zones and days spent reading Eddie's emails.

"You're so relaxed," she says, and gives me a quizzical look. She waits to see if I say more.

My onscreen life stays private, but I give her this: "You'd be surprised how good it feels to breathe out."

She nods, understanding at least part of what I'm saying, and watches me climb back to my tower room—where correspondence awaits.

When I wake up the next day with Eddie's words nesting comfortably in my brain (*you just might be everything I've ever looked for*) and head to the shower, I feel at last as if my sickness is gone and my heartache is lifted. But as the hot water hits my head and steam gathers on the shower door, the reality of what I've done strikes me full force.

Oh my God. Oh my God. Breathe in, breathe out—forget that. I have committed a big lie. Two big lies. More than that. And the worst part about it is—

"I'm kind of happy," I admit to Hanna as she steams up

a latte for me before our early-morning *Word* meeting. I felt the need for a post-illness coffee fix, plus some sage advice that only a woman in leg warmers and a 1980s aerobic outfit (think wedgie and spandex) can give.

"But you're not happy about deceiving him, are you?" Hanna leans onto the counter and passes me the caramel syrup. Normally I'm a purist, just coffee and milk, but today I'm in dire need of sweetening—both drinkwise and otherwise.

"Of course I don't want to be lying. Not to him." I think of Leyla's friendly smile, all the help she's been giving me at the *Word* while I've been absent. "And I feel terrible about *her*. Except that I'm trying to help her—"

"You *were* trying," Hanna correct. She arranges wooden stir-sticks into neon plastic cups and shakes her head. "One time, on *Life's a Beach*, we did this episode where my character got a love note from someone—they didn't tell us who it was, for real, at least not until the end of the show. Anyway, I wanted it to be from this guy Lyle, but it ended up being from Brian, who I had kissed once at a party and it was gross, but that's another story."

I stare at her as the words rush out. "Um, not to be rude or anything..." If I were in editing mode, I would have trimmed that whole thing she said to find a point somewhere.

"I know, you have school, and you're late, and you're wondering why I told you that." I nod at her. She adjusts the straps on her electric blue leotard. "It struck me as odd, after that show ended, that even though it was made up, even though I was just playing a character, I still had an opinion. That I said the words someone wrote for me and acted—as much as teen drama shows have acting—as though I didn't care who the note came from. But really, I did. And it would have been so much better, for the show, for me, if I'd just done what I felt." She stares at me with one of her cut-to-commercial looks, all poignant and deep.

"So basically, I have to come clean is what you're saying." I secure the plastic lid and sip my latte, dread building inside where only yesterday I had felt pure excitement.

"I can't tell you what to do." Hanna shrugs. "But I can tell you this: no real friendship or relationship can survive too much deceit." She pauses. "And in light of that, I should tell you that I didn't make that up. It's an old *Life's a Beach* line." She grins apologetically. "I still know the scripts. Sorry."

"Hey," I say back as I'm halfway out the door, "even the best of us use other people's words."

As if on cue, I get to the *Word* office (eight minutes late, which for a normal person is okay but for me, hyper-vigilant and punctual Cyrie, is way off base) just in time to hear Mr. Reynolds give his monthly warnings about plagiarizing.

"All I can say is—don't!" He glances at me and then at

the clock as I slide into a seat across from Leyla, who kicks me under the table as a welcome back. Linus signs *hi* and I nod to him, wondering if his crush is still intact or if he's thought better of it by now. If someone isn't returning your affections, how long do you let it go on, really?

"So, in closing, quote where you need to, and be original in both your wording and your choice of subject matter, and you'll be well on your way toward the journalistic greatness we strive for."

For which we strive, I think, placing the preposition where it's meant (according to my sources) to go.

The meeting continues with a rundown of all the things I've missed, and the spread for the week. Leyla's voice bubbles with pride. "It's all done. The paper's complete. I did the layout and worked on some of the photo captions." She looks at me, and I realize she wants my opinion.

"That's great," I tell her and study the pictures. She's done exactly as she should—clear captions, names spelled correctly, exciting leads. All without my help. I swallow hard. "You're really . . . you did it." My voice lacks luster, but not because there's anything wrong with what she's done.

"You don't like it?" Her face is worried.

I stand up and force myself to sound enthusiastic, when all I can do I wish I'd never turned on my computer and started the marathon back-and-forth with Eddie. Not that

I started it. He did. Only, I answered. "No, no. It's really good, Leyla. Seriously. You are really capable."

Satisfaction spreads across her face. "Thanks."

"Yeah, she totally pulled everything together this week." Linus hands me a piece of paper. "That's the printout that went home with every Weston student a few days ago. See? It even mentions the make-your-own-mix for the grab bag. We'll email a reminder to everyone, too. But some people like to have paper, you know . . . " He stutters for a second and looks at me.

Is he nervous? I try to remain professional despite the myriad issues brewing. "Well, I can't tell you how much I appreciate all the help." I make my voice louder so every-one in the room will hear. "I hate being sick. And, well, just thanks for all the efforts to make this office run smoothly while I was gone."

"It wasn't easy," Mr. Reynolds acknowledges. "What with you and Rox away."

Hearing the mention of his name brings back his emails . . . *everything I've ever looked for, can't you feel it? . . . you make me smile even when I'm sleeping.* I do my best to put on a good face.

Jill Carnegie, making one of her rare appearances, inter-rupts my attempts by saying, "I'm still waiting for one last donation. Cyrie—this one might interest you."

I turn to her as the rest of the room shuffles about their

business. "Oh yeah? We could use another vacation spot." I think about Wendy's lakeside cabin, how pristine it is, how much I've always wanted to go. How I probably never will.

"This is way better than Wendy's." Jill smirks at me and lowers her voice just enough that she doesn't draw attention to our conversation. She tilts her head and gives a fake smile. "The medical offices at Pinehurst—you know the ones, right?" She doesn't wait for me to nod, but of course I do know the ones, since that's where Dr. Schnoz is located. "Well, my father golfs with one of the dentists there..." Phew, dentists. Teeth. "And, long story short—we might get a free nose job for the auction!"

This last part she squeals out with excitement—loud enough that everyone turns to hear her, to see me hear the news—and, just as this scene is unfolding, who should walk in, just in time to take it all in, but Eddie.

Crouched over the computer screen with Linus, Leyla doesn't see him come in, but when Mr. Reynolds calls, "Rox! Back so soon?" Leyla turns to see him. He stands there, torn, it seems, between helping me out of my jam with Jill (whose smirk is enough to warrant an anvil dropped on her head) and waltzing over to Leyla. He looks back and forth between us.

Finally, I take matters into my own hands—or mouth. "Jill, why don't you see if you can get the doctors' offices to donate shrink time, and that way you can bid on it and see if perhaps double sessions a week might undo some of the damage your psyche sustained when your dad decided long ago to spend more time on the golf course than with his own daughter."

Jill's face crumbles. Defeat. Match point—me.

Except, as soon as I've accomplished this, Eddie turns away from me, toward Leyla. She manages to hug him without barfing, or the aid of a ghost sheet, and then walks over to me, calling for a conference in The Heap.

"He's back?" I ask as we huddle amidst the papers and old coffee mugs while Eddie confers with Mr. Reynolds.

She lowers her eyes and voice. "He missed me."

He missed her. He missed her because of me. "Don't sound so thrilled," I tell her. I want to offer her comfort, but I can't take my eyes off Eddie. He looks different. Not entirely changed, but something in his walk. Maybe just being apart from him makes me see him differently. Or maybe it was our exchange of words. I look at Leyla. "What?"

"You keep staring at him," she says. She picks at her cuticles and bites a nail.

"No. It's just—why'd … um … it's just an adjustment being back after missing so many days."

Leyla crosses her arms, watching me, and then watching the rest of the room. Linus calls over to her, "What do you want to do about that last piece?"

Leyla touches my shoulder. "Look, I gotta finish this. But … just talk to him, okay?"

My worry about all the emails combines with anger. "What now?"

"Jeez—don't be so pissy. I'm covering for you," Leyla motions to the paper. "You cover for me. Just for now."

"What exactly am I meant to say this time?" I ask. I want the security of my warm bed, the even warmer words rolling back and forth between us.

Leyla sees Eddie look over at us and blushes. "Just tell him..." She looks at me as my own face reddens. His words. His letters. Already I know I will stay up way too late rereading everything we've written, stashing everything in an "old drafts" file that Leyla will never look at. I will say how I missed him, too. How she did. "I'm sure you'll think of something."

The truth is, I have lots to say to Eddie—but not as Leyla. Just as myself. And I have lots to say to Leyla, but I can't. I'm caught in the editorial position of having expressed myself so much that I can't edit it off the page. As Leyla catches me looking at Eddie and Linus stares at me over the top of the screen, I wonder if maybe I'm better off saying—and doing—nothing.

Luckily, the bell rings, and we are herded out of the room and off on our separate ways to class.

seventeen

So you still haven't said anything?" Hanna holds thick brown paper over the windows of Any Time Now and waves her hand so I'll give her the masking tape.

"You're changing the décor again? So soon?" I ask, avoiding her question. I haven't said or done anything about the "situation," as I've come to think of it. Yesterday, in my last consultation with Dr. Schnoz before the big session in January, I was so distracted that I didn't even ask to try on the latest Hollywood nose—a perfectly angled slope with tapered nostrils.

"You know what word I hate?" I continue, handing her

the tape. Hanna queries me with her eyebrows. "*Nostrils*," I tell her. "It's such an odd sound." She looks at me as though I'm speaking gibberish, and I shrug, distracted yet again.

Two weeks have come and gone in a muddle of homework, yoga sessions with my parents to get them off my back about said "situation" (I've only said that I feel "plagued" by the last of my college essay questions), and a few scattered conversations with Leyla. She's been busy with SATs and the paper, and Linus and I have only been signing across the room. And though I've managed to control myself, I did check the Sumbodee email account (twice—okay, three times) and there's nothing new there. As for Eddie, I've seen him around a little, and even went for an impromptu run around the track with him. With just our footsteps pounding and our breaths coming in jagged, cold bursts, it was easy to imagine that I could tell him. Admit everything. But I didn't. We'd ended the run with a sweaty hug, but in the cold air, the heat soon turned to a chill.

"How come you're not sticking with all the hair band fun of the late 1980s?"

"Bored with it. I need inspiration for an audition." Hanna papers the window and the room darkens. Tables are upended, chairs stacked, props boxed up for storage.

"You're auditioning?"

She shrugs. "No biggie. Just a pilot."

"But you said you were done with acting—"

"And I was. Until now. At some point you gotta just come out of hiding." She stands on a chair and looks down at me. "Which brings me back to my first question."

"Okay, no. I didn't say anything. I wanted to. Leyla's just...she seems confused, too. Or maybe distracted by all her work. Did I tell you she got promoted at the paper? After I was absent she took on more responsibility. Mr. Reynolds decided she should have more control, so she's a staff writer and head of layout."

Hanna hops down, wearing the roll of masking tape as a bracelet. "Which is great for her. Maybe she'll use her journalistic persona to—" she puts on a voice-over drama voice "—uncover the truth about what's really happening at Weston High."

"Nothing's been happening. I mean, Leyla's been doing her thing, I've been working on applications, and Eddie's been..." I breathe in, thinking of his voice, his latest funny improv in Drama. "It's been normal. Ish."

"Ish."

"Except for the fact that Leyla and Eddie hold hands in the hallways and I want to die looking at them." I feel tears start. They well up in my eyes, but don't spill over.

"It should be you, huh?" Hanna's voice is soothing, her face kind.

I nod, admitting it all. "He's in love with me." I let out one sob. "He just thinks it's her." The dim light echoes in my insides. "And I just...I can't deal with either of them because of it. I'm terrible."

"You're not terrible. You're flawed. Like we all are." Hanna nods in the paper-darkened room. "Looks like you have a chance to say something right now, if you want."

Outside the glass front door of Any Time Now, her face blocked by the *closed* sign, is Leyla. I recognize her flats and the pink scarf that dangles down to her knees.

The pretty fall is gone now, and the cold, depressing fall is left in its place...the short days, the end of something. When I open the door and see Leyla's face, I feel nervous.

"Hey, come on in." Hanna leaves us to sit on two bright orange plastic chairs while she goes into the back to keep packing things up. Who knows what theme will come out next, what time period will strike her fancy.

Leyla and I sit with our feet propped on the metal railing that rims the room, carefully tilting back in our chairs. "You know I'm gonna wind up on my butt," she says, and laughs.

"Don't worry," I tell her. "I'll help you up."

We sit in semi-comfortable quiet until Leyla puts her chair flat on the floor and sighs. "Actually, I think you've done that enough."

I keep tilting, daring myself back, and look at her. "What do you mean?"

Leyla stands up, pacing. I stay seated, watching her. "The thing is...it's just..." Her shoulders slump; she turns her face toward the floor, her voice warbling. "You did so much for me, you know? And I wish..."

I stand up, my stomach churning. Did she say something to Eddie? Of course I figured he'd mention the emails to her, but I figured she'd just assume he meant the old ones. But as I think this, I realize that maybe Leyla's not the one who's being slow to catch on—maybe it's me. Maybe Leyla does read the sent messages, or the files on the account. I'm so caught up in my own feelings that I've underestimated the area in which she excels—knowing me.

"It's pretty obvious." Leyla turns to face me, her arms across her chest.

"What is?" I ask, playing dumb.

She stomps her foot. "Don't, Cyrie."

I pretend to study the wall, the empty spaces where the Wham! and Duran Duran posters used to be. "Just to be clear, we're talking about—"

"You like Rox."

"Eddie," I say automatically, and then really wish I could pull the word back inside my mouth.

Leyla swivels, annoyed. "His name's Rox. Everyone calls him that and you know it. And you also know by now that we're breaking up." Her voice loses its edge.

I watch her face for tears, but none come. "Oh, I'm sorry." And I really am. "What can I do?"

"That's what I'm saying," she tells me. "You did enough.

You know, I probably shouldn't even have been with him in the first place. I mean, it's not like we have much in common. It's my own dumb fault for not seeing it before—all of this."

Listening to her, I assume she means that since she got so nervous around him—nervous enough to vomit—maybe that wasn't a good omen for a long-term relationship. HOW-EVER, I suddenly think in Eddie's all-caps, if they break up, I won't have any reason to email Eddie anymore. Everything will go back to the way it was. Except, not. "But you like each other."

"No," she eyes me, face-on. "That's what I'm saying." She waits and clamps her mouth shut, the seconds ticking by. She points at me, which sets my insides bubbling—this is due to a lifetime of people pointing for only one reason. Leyla is going to bring up my nose, now? I wait, but she doesn't. Instead, with her finger still outstretched, she says, *"You* like him."

Now it's my turn to feel nauseated. If Leyla or anyone on the staff used the cliché "the truth hurts," I'd make them do a rewrite. But here, in the empty, timeless café, it's all I can think of. I can't even offer a rebuttal. I stand up, my feet about a foot apart as though I'm about to sprint, which is maybe what I want to do but can't. I sit down.

To her credit, Leyla doesn't poke or prod with words. She just lets me wait out the silence.

Finally, after what feels like an hour but is probably only

one-tenth of that, Hanna materializes with tea for two. One mug is an '80s remnant with *Who's the Boss?* written across it and the other is left over from the Victorian tea house era—with delicate roses and a gilt-edged saucer. Nothing matches on the tray in front of us—plastic spoons and intricate silver forks for the salad she's thoughtfully prepared—and nothing matches my visions of how things should go, either. Hanna's even included ginger biscuits and honey cream, which she knows I love, but I can't eat a bite.

Leyla takes a cookie and eats it, still waiting, the crumbs nestling into the soft fuzz of her peach-hued sweater.

"How long have you known?" My eyes find hers, my whole self feels rattled. It's easy to know what to say when someone insults me—how to get back at them—but it's near-impossible to know how to dig myself out of this pit. At least I don't have to tell her about the emails now.

"Not that long," she says and chews. "But maybe I knew all along, if that makes sense?" She sounds like herself now, same lilting voice, same gentle manner.

"I couldn't tell you," I say, and realize how futile it sounds.

Leyla pours some tea for both of us but doesn't drink hers. "Remember that column I did last year? The one about janitorial expenses?" I nod. "You underlined when I used the word *couldn't*." She adds milk to the tea. "You said I meant *wouldn't*. There's a difference."

It occurs to me how much Leyla has listened to me

during the course of our friendship, how much advice I've offered, even if understated, and that maybe—"You don't think I *made* you date him, do you?"

Leyla raises her eyebrows. Clearly I'm touching on something she's already considered. "It's possible."

I inhale deeply. "Okay. So I liked him. But I really don't think I meant for you to be with him as a sort of extension of me..."

"HOWEVER," we both say, and while maybe it would have been funny a few weeks ago, now we don't laugh.

Leyla drops a cube of sugar into her cup and I wonder why she bothers getting it ready if she's not going to drink it. "But that's what I became, you know?" Her eyes find mine. "Not really me liking a guy, more like me semi-liking a guy and you closing the deal. You making it go farther than it probably would have."

What if I hadn't facilitated their getting to know each other? What if they'd just had little crushes that passed?

"I'm sorry," I say.

"Are you apologizing because you lied to me, or because I figured it out?" Leyla's voice has the edge again. An edge that doesn't suit her.

"I'm sorry for the emails," I tell her. I picture the full inbox, my contentedness at seeing a new message in bold print.

She shrugs. "Those are old news. We haven't done that for over a month."

A month? I think back. Eddie's college trip was only a couple of weeks ago. "Not really a month."

"Fine—five weeks."

Five weeks? I study her face. She doesn't know about the barrage of emails exchanged while Eddie was gone. Leyla's still in the dark about that? A mix of shivers and sweat run their course down my back. "How'd you figure it out, any-way?" I wonder how she possibly could have not checked the account. I guess if you're losing interest in someone, you stop trying to find out about them.

"When he came back," she answers me. "That look you had on your face when he came into the *Word* room. It was like..." She pauses, searching for the correct word or phrase. "It was like you'd found something you'd lost." She coughs. "I had a hunch even before then. At Halloween. I kept thinking that maybe you wished you were under my sheet instead of yours."

"Because I didn't wear a costume?"

"No, that was just you being determined to be left out," she says, her mouth twisted and sad. "I knew because, even though you're a great writer and editor and can think on your feet, you really knew just what to say to him outside in the moonlight. It was like you'd practiced. In your head."

I look at my hands, wishing they'd stayed clasped with Eddie's in that Drama box, that things in the light were the same as they were in the dark. "I had." I look at Leyla for support, for understanding. But what I get back is—

"I've thought a lot about this, Cyrie. And the thing is, it's not right. What we did wasn't right—but what you're doing is worse."

Good thing she doesn't know about the most recent emails or she'd be even more disappointed. My chest feels weighted with all those secreted words.

"What can I do?" I ask her with my hands out. "How can I make it better?"

"If our friendship means anything, you'll give me a little space," she says. She pulls her hair away from her face and looks away.

"I can do that," I say. I'm used to being alone by now.

"And..." She stands up. "You can tell him."

I drop my teacup onto the floor. Hanna appears with a broom and busies herself like an extra on a film—no interaction with us, just doing her job. "No way."

"You have to," Leyla insists. "Not for me. Not for him. For you."

I shake my head. Telling Eddie the truth would ruin everything. If he knew how much I liked him, he'd never even go running with me—not even in the wintery dusk. "I can't."

Leyla looks angry. She coughs and heads for the door, leaving me with broken shards and spilled milk and this question: "Cyrie? How can you even look at yourself in the mirror?"

eighteen

People always think that the hallways of school are where everything happens. Love by the lockers, brawls in the halls. Or in homeroom. Or the girls' bathroom. But all those places are nothing when compared to the ultimate place to observe student life: under the bleachers.

I'm jogging in place to keep warm as I wait for Eddie. This will be our second time meeting here to go running, and I've been running after school every day to prepare my lungs for the icy chill I'll battle when trying to keep up with him. Now, out here in the cold, my feet pounding the ground, it's almost easy to forget what Leyla wants me to do.

Not telling Eddie feels as normal as slipping into a well-worn sweatshirt—cozy and, yes, safe.

To my left is a couple engaged in what could only properly be called mouth-wrestling; to my right is a cluster of disillusioned drama-bes who didn't make the cut for *Guys and Dolls*, the winter musical.

"I should've been cast as Sarah!" One girl wails. "I'm totally pure and good-natured."

"Well, I'm much better at Adelaide than she is," another intones, letting a few lines slide out in song.

"Whatever, you guys, I'm freezing," says another, and I wish I had the *Word* camera to snap a shot of them bemoaning. I could submit it as a candid for the paper and Leyla could come up with a good caption. Or she would, if we were speaking, which we aren't really, because I can't bring myself to tell Eddie anything and she won't go back on her speech at Any Time Now.

"Ready?" Eddie asks, his hands shoved into his gloves. He looks at the drama girls and says in a newscaster voice, "More downhearted Westies wonder if next time will be their shot at the stage."

"Story at eleven," I say. His cheeks are ruddy, and he claps his hands together to ward off the chill.

"Aren't you going to be cold?" He motions to my head and I instinctively flinch, as though he's pointing to my nose. He dodges it, though, and taps my head. "A hat would be useful."

"True," I say, stretching with one leg in front of the other. "Next time."

"Right," he says, confirming that there will be one. "You're the only one who's daring enough to jog in this weather. The rest of the guys are in the weight room."

"Yeah, I'm pretty tough." I try not to focus on being grouped with the rest of his teammates, with "the guys" and the thick-skinned sporty Westies. Then I think about something. "I'm not 'daring.'"

Eddie grins and raises his eyebrows. "No?"

I couldn't be. Daring means you're willing to risk something—and I'm decidedly against risking these runs, or our friendship, or even embarrassment, by risking the truth. Although in some ways, every day I leave the house is a risk. I shrug.

"I'll give you a head start."

I shake my head. "No, thanks. I don't need one."

We run side by side along the track and then, without discussing it, veer off the path and into the woods. The frozen ground makes for a heavy impact and I feel it in my knees— but not half as much as I do when Eddie slows down, then stops.

Surrounded by trees emptied of their leaves, he turns to me. "Couldn't you just stay right here for, like, ever?"

"'Like,' ever?" I put my hand over my mouth. "Please excuse my edits. Really." I shake my head.

"Not *like* ever. Just ever." He laughs. "Don't go changing your editorial ways for me."

We stand there, breathing hard in the winter air, our cheeks flushed, my nose probably Rudolph-red and just as prominent.

"Do you miss her?" I ask him, wondering if it's a mistake to bring Leyla up when I'm alone with him.

He shrugs. "Do you? You're never together anymore. I used to think you guys were inseparable."

I nod. "Yeah, I do miss her. A lot."

"What happened?" He leans on a tree and crosses his arms. His sweatshirt is faded and stretched out at the hem. I could fit in there with him.

"Just ... we had a disagreement. That's all."

He sticks his chin out as a nod. "It happens."

"What exactly happened with you two?" I ask as though I don't know. Even pairing them in the sentence makes my stomach flip. "You don't have to say if you don't want to."

"Did you ever hear a song on the radio and think, oh I am so going home right now to download it?" I nod. He continues. "And then you do, and theoretically you should be psyched, right? I mean, here is this song you heard and wanted to—you know—own, right away. But then ... "

I think about the discarded songs, the times I made the

same mistake. "Then you listen to it again and it's like the magic isn't there. You thought this chord or that lyric was so incredible, but then it wasn't."

Eddie leaves his tree perch and comes right over to me. My heart flails. He hugs me. If only he would see beyond this moment, see that I am the person in the song he wanted. Or, I am the song.

"I wish it could've been like it was in the emails she and I wrote to each other. But maybe that's the problem. Some things don't translate off the page." I nod. He hugs me and into my ear says softly, "I'm lucky to have a friend like you, Cyrie."

A friend. One of the guys. Yeah. I swallow the cold air and my feelings, yet again, and follow him through the woods, back out onto the track.

ℓ

Post-Thanksgiving, I kick into overdrive, mailing off applications and, with Eddie, finalizing the auction—the programs, the donations, the newspaper edition.

"I can't believe it's this weekend," he says as we pour over the schedule again.

"Okay," I say to Mr. Reynolds. "It's finished."

"I'll take them to the printer," Mr. Reynolds says, leaving me and Eddie to close up the *Word* office. The final bell rang a while ago, and the once-crowded hallways are vacant save for a few dropped gloves and a stray scarf.

"How cool would it be to win the stuff on this list?" Eddie asks, eyeing the auction list.

"I know. Lifetime supply of donuts?"

Eddie points to an item. "No—downloads for life. I'd take that."

"Have you made your mix for the grab bag?" My mother sewed a giant pumpkin-colored sack for us to keep by the door—everyone who puts a CD in can take one out.

Eddie nods. "Of course. Led off with a little Van Halen and segued into classic Lou Reed. Can't go wrong with a little Van, though."

I nod back. "I spent way too long compiling a playlist. Way too long." I stare at him, wanting to go over in minute detail each song I chose and why, and how, really, the mix is for him—but it's one I'll never give to him. I'll drop it into the anonymous pumpkin bag and it will be picked up by some random person—and perhaps never listened to.

"So you're hoping to bid on some Weston wonders—let me guess, a cup of tea at Any Time Now?"

"Could be good," I say and tidy up around me as though neatening things up in the office will clarify my insides. "Or, maybe I'll go for Wendy Von Schmedler's cabin," I say, wistful at the thought of it. "I know it's great in summer—or so

I've heard—but I think winter would be even better. Fireside, skating, hot chocolate."

Eddie agrees. "If you've got pockets deep enough."

I shake my head. "Actually, I'm not bidding at all."

"Nothing worth your money?" Eddie queries while digging through his backpack.

"Nothing money can buy," I say and then wish I hadn't. What if he thinks I mean something by it? Even if I do, I don't want him catching on. He doesn't react.

I continue my organizational mission, chucking out slips of paper we don't need and wondering if anyone will bid on my auction item. "You think they will?" I ask him.

"I don't see why not," Eddie says. "Seems like there are a lot of people who would want your help writing something." He looks at me.

Every once in a while I wonder what he'd do if I just told him. Came right out and said *hey, I was the one who wrote all those emails—the good ones, anyway. The ones you like. The ones you couldn't shake off.* Or, I wonder if maybe he knows. I lock eyes with him, to ask him that non-verbal question. But he just looks back at me and asks, "What? Do I have something on my chin? I had that soggy Eggplant Parmesan for lunch. Big mistake."

I laugh, pushing aside my thoughts. The CD that's playing switches over to a mix I made for Leyla last year. "Oh, I love this song!" I sing along for a few seconds and Eddie mouths the words. People bring in their CDs and end up leaving them here. We use them for coasters, or keep playing them until they're worn out.

"Never would have taken you for a Neil Diamond fan," Eddie says, full of mock scolding.

"Don't ever doubt the Diamond," I say. "'Forever in Blue Jeans' is one of the greatest songs ever written."

"Story at eleven," Eddie comments. "Is that song on your grab-bag mix?"

"Nope." I keep singing.

He does a silly dance and I do one, too, lost in the music and the emptiness of the room, that loose feeling that takes over once you've completed all the work you can do on a project.

We're laughing and in mid-dance when the door opens. Jockorama Josh charges in with Leyla in tow. She's holding his hand but not looking too thrilled about it. She eyes me and Eddie and gets closer to Josh, who pulls her under his arm protectively.

"Hey." Josh gives Eddie the guy nod. Eddie runs his hands through his hair and nods back.

"I think we're all set," I say to Eddie and busy myself with piling papers as the song ends. Leyla looks at me, her eyes questioning. *Did you tell him?*

Eddie grabs his jacket and heads for the door with his

backpack slung over one shoulder. "See you guys at the auction, I guess?"

Leyla sighs, knowing I haven't. Josh rummages through a file near The Heap and I whisper to Leyla, "I can't."

She holds up her hands. "Forget it, Cyrie." She glances over her shoulder at Josh. "I thought you were different, you know, back when we became friends? You seemed so confident, so much like you couldn't care less what other people thought. But it turns out I was wrong."

"No—I am that way," I hiss back to her.

"You aren't. You just want to be." She crosses her arms over her chest. She's wearing the Wendy Von Schmedler group uniform, designer duds and matching accessories.

"Oh, and you're back with Josh? That's original."

Leyla looks at me with the kind of look that Wendy gives me whenever I enter a room—like I've degraded the whole place. "At least I have someone."

I can't believe things have sunk so low with Leyla that we're throwing insults at each other. "I thought *you* were different," I tell her. "Not like them." I thumb at Josh as though he represents the entire Wendy crowd, the PBVs, except not just vapid. Thoughtless and mean as well.

"Guess we're both disappointed," she says. When Josh returns to her side, she takes off.

Despite the neat room and the tidied table, I don't feel any less cluttered inside.

nineteen

It's a huge success!" Mr. Reynolds beams at the *Word* staff. "This auction is the best in Weston High history. And I'm not just saying that."

"Come on, you probably say that every year," I reply. We're clustered by the apple cider in the far corner of the barn, making sure that the tallies are correct, that people are paying by cash or check, that no one forgets to bid high and bid often.

Our setup really is pretty spectacular. Bales of hay spill from a huge wooden wagon, pumpkins dot the windowsills, bright fall leaves crunch underfoot, and the air smells like cinnamon (thanks to freshly baked sticky rolls from Any Time

Now). Wilson Farms is a vision of autumnal glory—caramel apples and scarecrows, wreaths and cornucopias bursting with produce.

"We're raking it in with the sporting goods," Josh says, his eyes on the bidding list in front of him, but his hand is on Leyla's shoulder. She sits next to him, subdued.

"And with the beauty and spa offerings, too!" Jill shows us the sheet.

"I was worried people would bail on the grab bag," Mr. Reynolds points to the pumpkin-shaped bag set to the side of the entryway.

"But people are really taking part," Linus says.

I glance over at it, wondering which bag, box, or pocket my CD will go into tonight. At the evening's end I'll close my eyes and dip my hand in among the plastic covers, hoping for the best—whatever that means.

People mill around, eyeing the items, wandering from table to table as the silent auction continues. I walk around, ignoring my guilt about Leyla and wondering where Eddie is. When I spot him jotting something down, I go over to see. He's putting in a bid on one of the auction items, entering his name on an already filled-up sheet. (I always feel bad for the places like Mr. LawnCare, which has no bids at all.)

"The lake house?" I ask.

"I thought it'd be a good graduation party place." Then he explains. "Not like I was stealing it from you…"

I shrug. "You can't steal something that someone doesn't have, right?" And I don't have it—or him—or my friend. "How come no one bids for Mr. LawnCare? I mean, everyone has a lawn that needs care." I've put just a bit too much emphasis on this and close my mouth, afraid to be revealed.

"See? You didn't have to worry," Eddie says, pointing to another paper.

I don't know if he means about being lonely, or him not returning my feelings. Turns out he means neither. "Linus bid—and won." Eddie picks up the clipboard that has my auction item attached. The time limit for bidding on it has expired, and Linus' name is circled in red as the final—and highest—bidder.

"Looks that way," I say. I should feel good about it, but it only adds to my confusion. The past few weeks have made me lonelier than ever—with Leyla retreating and Eddie and me hanging out as much as we have. I wouldn't trade the time with him, it's only that I know it doesn't mean to him what it means to me. You'd think that just being with him would be enough. It used to be. Only now, it feels only part real, as though I'm playing hide and seek and waiting to be found.

The letters were so much easier. I look at his hands and think about his fingers on the keyboard, typing to me when he thought he was typing to her. Maybe the solution is to reread the emails tonight and see if I still feel the same way.

The auction continues, with parents bidding and students

dressed up, and Wendy Von Schmedler's brother's band playing covers of songs that don't deserve replaying, as we raise thousands of dollars for the scholarship fund.

"You should all be very proud of yourselves," Mr. Reynolds says when the night is drawing to a close.

"We got it!"

Shrieks come in a wave from Wendy and her groupies. "Can you say New Year's?" she asks Jill.

Jill nods. "New Year's!"

"It wasn't a command." Wendy rolls her eyes. Announcing for the entire world (or at least those gathered at Wilson Farms) to hear, she says, "New Year's Eve—my house. At the lake."

"You bid on your own house?" Leyla asks, more incredulous than confused.

"Are you as thick as you seem?" Wendy laughs. Josh laughs, too.

"She wasn't being thick." My voice is stern. "It's just—it's your own house, so why bother paying for it?"

Wendy tosses her hair. "Out of school spirit." Can't argue with that. Maybe Wendy's got more charity in her than I thought. She smooths her dress. "Plus, I don't want someone else calling the shots up there. The lake house is my turf." She shoots me a look. "Of course, everyone's invited."

"Everyone with an invite, you mean," Leyla says, standing up. She pries Josh's arms from hers and defends me like I defended her.

"Of course," Wendy snorts. She looks at me and shakes her head, letting me know that yet again I will not be on her special list.

"Don't you know? Invites are so last year." Leyla grins at me and goes to check on the desserts.

I'm impressed with Leyla's retort, with her defending me, even if it doesn't wind up scoring me an invite. I don't need to go, but I do need Leyla. I find her by the individual cups of pumpkin pudding no one seems to want to ingest.

"Thanks for that," I tell her, and try a bite of the mushy stuff because I feel bad for it. Yes, I have special feelings for inanimate objects. Then again, it doesn't take a therapist to figure out that perhaps I identify with the pumpkin pudding. "Am I like this gross stuff?" I offer Leyla a bite and she shakes her head.

"You know you're not." She takes a piece of carrot cake and forks some into her mouth. The frosting sticks to her lip. "I'm so glad that, you know, everything worked out."

I nod, then wonder exactly what she means. "With the invitation thing?"

She shakes her head. "No, with you finally—FINALLY— telling him."

The noise swirls around us, causing distractions and

jostling. I try a bite-sized piece of pumpkin bread. "Telling who what?"

Leyla leans in. "What'd he say when you told him? Rox. I'm sure he—"

I put the pudding down and look at her. I can't help but focus on the misplaced frosting. "I didn't ... I just—"

"I thought I saw you with him tonight." She tugs at her hair. "You were talking so close I just thought—"

I shake my head, my eyes sorry. "It's never gonna happen. What would he say? It would ruin everything. And it's better to just keep—" I want to say *friendship* or *things the way they are*, but Leyla interrupts.

"Keep the fantasy?" She pushes back from me, our closeness evaporating yet again. "No way. You think you're playing it safe, Cyrie, but really you're worse than all those fake girls you hate so much." She looks over her shoulder, at the Schmedler in her party-planning revelry.

"I don't hate them, I just—"

"Pity them?" Leyla's eyes are ablaze, her cheeks flushed. "Now I see why."

Back at home, I can't believe I thought Leyla and I were back on track after our weeks of growing silence. I want to call her and say sorry, but I don't know why I have to apologize to her for living my life the way I want. She can't make decisions for me. I never asked her to do that. Besides, if she's with Josh, she's hardly one to talk about doing the right thing.

All I have for consolation tonight is an unmarked CD I grabbed from the mix bag on the way out of the auction. I did check to make sure mine wasn't left behind, and it was in fact pocketed by some Westie who will hopefully find a new appreciation for Depeche Mode, the Smiths, the Cure, and even Neil Diamond (after hearing "Forever in Blue Jeans" in the *Word* room, I just had to sprinkle some in; too many people don't know the Diamond's magic).

I trudge up to my room and slide the new CD into my stereo, expecting greatness. The first song's not bad, some up-tempo tune about a girl with "mahogany hair." Usually new music makes me feel better, but this doesn't. My melancholy mood isn't even alleviated by the success of the auction, of all that hard work paying off. As I wander around my familiar surroundings, I suddenly realize why: all those hours, the frantic planning, the meetings, the jocular idea sessions—they're done. No more auction sessions with Eddie. Once the snow falls, no more running. And what else? No Leyla. No Leyla, no Eddie—at least, not the way I want him.

I just want things back the way they were—with Leyla being my friend and Eddie being the friend-that-I-want-to-become-more. All those words he and I exchanged, the visions I had of us. With a sigh, I decide that all I can do to quench my dreams is look at everything, all the correspondence, for the last time. All the emails all in a row. Once more. And then say goodbye to them. My mother always says not to live in the past, and maybe this is one step I can take to move forward.

I sit at my desk with my feet tucked under, longing for the familiar fonts, the words I've come to rely on. I'll log on, reread the emails in the Sumbodee account—for the last time. I will print them (just for my own benefit) and delete all evidence of the extra correspondence Eddie and I had. We'll put the past in its place.

In my comfy pajamas and a sweatshirt Eddie lent me after running last week, I log on to my regular email and find nothing except an "incomplete" notice from the college counselor, who insists that I must complete the essay about my greatest flaw by Monday. I sigh about that, and feel my insides swirl when I think about rereading Eddie's letters. I turn my printer on, ready to keep safe the words I've cherished.

Only, when I log on to the Sumbodee account, my pulse races—things aren't the way they should be. The account is blank. My heart dips in my chest, my fingers shake. The emails are gone. Everything I've saved is nowhere to be found. In its place is just a single, unread message:

> *Just when I was about to call you and say*
> *sorry about the auction, I find out about*

this. How could you keep this from me?
Don't I mean anything to you?

I'm short of breath. First I think it's from Eddie. Then, with growing pangs, I realize it's from Leyla. That she checked the account, erased everything, and left this for me. I wonder if I should write back. If I do, she'll know I was lame enough to log on again. If I don't, how will I repair—or try to repair— the damage I've done?

I stare at the screen for ages. Then I lie in bed, my heart as empty as the email account—devoid of all the words I worked so hard for, all the feelings I tried to hide and then revealed.

twenty

Winter comes on when I'm not looking. Drifts of light snow replace the fall leaves, leaving a desolate landscape across the football fields. I walk home from school—alone yet again—and stare at the empty goals. Up ahead, on their way to the diner, a group of PBVs giggle, their pom-pom hats bobbing as they walk.

"It's going to be awesome!"

"And she's getting, like, two bands and—"

"Catering by that fancy place in New York!"

I can tell they're referring to the New Year's Eve bash at Wendy's lake house. It's all anyone seems to be discussing lately—who will get an invitation and who won't. There's not a doubt in my mind that my locker will be on the "no" list. Without Leyla pulling for me, what little hope I had for attending seems to have vanished. I kick my boots along the sidewalk and try to make myself feel better by remembering Wendy's Halloween party, how silly it was, and unfun, with everyone talking and dancing and my own costumeless state. Her bathroom had more beauty products than a department store.

I could head to Any Time Now but it's still closed for refurbishments, so I go instead toward Main Street to browse for holiday gifts and any last-minute inspiration for my one remaining essay. I bypass WAJS radio station, ignore Buggy's Gifts, and find myself in the Apothecary, amid the vials of perfume and the shelves stocked with bubblegum body balm and mint foot scrub. And lipsticks. Maybe I need some makeup to cover my "greatest flaw," and then I'd know what to say.

The racks of gloss and eyeliner, eye pencils and complexion corrector are off to one side. Even though I'm not a makeup person (I hardly need to draw more attention to my face), I go and investigate. Halfheartedly, I hold a foundation up to my arm, testing the color in the light.

"You're more of an ivory."

I turn and see Wendy Von Schmedler, complete with her trendy boots and straightened hair, her face made up so perfectly she looks as though she has no makeup on.

"If I need your help, I'll ask for it." I'm not in the mood for one of Wendy's fights. She picks them for the sake of hearing herself talk, and I'm too lonely, too forlorn, too everything to deal with her. A clerk passes by; he eyes both of us and gives me a smile. I put the cover-up back.

"You know, if you'd let go of the nose thing, you could actually be pretty."

I stare at her. "What?" Venom rises in me. "If you were any more shallow you'd be a puddle." I want to crack up, to tell someone my latest line, but I have no one to tell. Even Linus has been steering clear, saying he'll give me space until he calls in the auction item he bid on—otherwise known as Me.

Wendy looks at me with contempt, but then her mouth crumples. "I didn't say it to be mean. I meant it as … "

"Oh, a compliment? That's like me saying your bath-room has more beauty associated with it than you do—does that feel complimentary?" I say this and then, even though it's Wendy—mean Wendy, Wendy who has used every opportunity since fifth grade to torment, mock, and verbally mutilate me—I feel bad.

Instead of offering a retort, she slides her back down the cosmetics shelf and sits on the gray rug, looking up at me. Then she puts her head in her hands. "You're right."

"I'm—" I stop myself. I'm right? As in correct? As in— she's not going to pound me back? I look down at her creaseless outfit, her ironed hair, and wonder how long it took her to get ready this morning in that cavernous bathroom of hers. I picture her surrounded by her lotions and potions, peering into the mirror, wondering if the mirror really reflects who she is.

"Ugghh." A groan escapes from my mouth as I slide down next to her. Lipsticks tower over us, bottles of perfumes and products that promise to deliver but usually don't. "I'm sorry, Wendy. That was mean."

Wendy's face remains poised, but her eyes give away more. Then she speaks. "I always come here when I feel..." She looks around to make sure no one we know is watching.

"When you feel..." I raise my eyebrows but keep my voice soft.

"You know what's funny?" She looks over her shoulder. "Everyone would die hearing me say this, but—you and I? We're not that different."

True horror shows on my face. "I beg to differ."

Wendy fiddles with a bottle of foundation, turning it this way and that as she talks. "No. We're not. Maybe it comes from different places—like, you're this way because of..." She dips her head, casting her sorrowful eyes down toward the rug.

"Fine—because of the unnamed thing. The elephant in the room, AKA my nose." I sigh, wrapping and unwrapping my scarf around my hands. Wendy and I haven't spoken civilly in so many years it feels as though we're speaking some very foreign language—not French or Spanish, one not even offered at Weston High. "And just why are you the way you are?"

Wendy opens the bottle and tests the beige liquid on her wrist. "Mean, you mean?"

"Nice sentence." The words fly out and I flick myself as punishment. "Ignore that."

"See? That's something I would do." Wendy puts the bottle of foundation back on the rack, crosses her legs, and explains. "My mother is responsible for ninety percent of the makeup and other products I own, okay? She buys them and—" Wendy does air quotes here "—'gives' them to me as 'treats.' But the reality is, she's obsessed with crafting me into this persona. I need to be perfect to make her happy."

"And . . . " I study the bottle of makeup she just put back. "'Clarifying clean complexion foundation' is going to do that?"

She shrugs. Up close, through the blended blush, the expertly applied mascara, I see Wendy for who she really is: a girl who can't possibly be what other people want her to be. A girl who disappoints herself by trying. Ahem.

"All the makeup in the world, the scrubs and liquid-gold soap—two hundred bucks for point-four ounces, by the way—it's not going to make my mother happy. Because she's miserable. You've met her."

I think back to Mrs. Von Schmedler's appearance, her incarnations as a blonde, a redhead, the streaks careful and perfect. All her attempts at morphing into someone else. Someone younger. "You're not your mother," I say.

"And you're not your nose." She looks at me head-on, waiting for the fallout.

I bite the middle of my upper lip. "But I feel like I am." The clerk goes by again, sweeping up a few stray leaves, smiling at us. "Rude," I say under my breath. I look away.

"You're so quick to glare at people!" Wendy laughs. I want to punch her, but she's got a point.

"It's just defensiveness. Makes me good at sports."

"And bad at people." She looks over at the clerk. He's our age, probably a senior from nearby Guilford High. "Did it ever occur to you that everyone stares at everyone all the time? Not *just* at you—but *also* at you?"

I let her words sink in. "I guess not." Inside, I feel something stirring—not a comeback, not anything cruel, just a space. "Since we're sitting here, on the floor of the Apothecary, talking as though we don't despise each other, can I ask you something?"

Wendy tests another shade of foundation. "Go for it."

"What would happen if we weren't mean? It's not like I want to be, you know? It just happens."

"So it's out of your control?" She looks at me quizzically. "I don't buy that. You're the editor of the paper—you rocked varsity tennis, you do all this stuff. All this stuff that requires discipline and control." She screws the top back on the makeup. "I'm buying this one." She stands up. "See? I feel better already." She holds the product as though it's a key, ready to open doors and change things for her.

I stand up and follow her, feeling oddly serene. Maybe taking away meanness opens up room for something else. But what?

"That's it? We're done? All this psycho-drama-intense conversation, and now you're buying makeup?"

Wendy turns to me, her mouth placid, her eyes working on converting from sad to steely. "Every now and again I have a maternal meltdown. This one was caused by my mother's insistence that I 'get my skin in shape' before my New Year's party."

"Your skin's fine," I tell her, feeling sorrier for her than ever.

"Yeah, it's my attitude I have to work on!" She cracks us both up. I reach out to touch her arm—or, not hug her, but something—and she shakes her head. "Don't waste the effort on me, okay? I'm kind of on automatic, at least until I get the hell away from home and head out west for college." She grabs a handful of other items—tweezers, eye shadow, a glittery powder. "But you have potential, you know?" She grins. "Even if you have the biggest damn nose in the history of the world."

Our eyes lock. I could—I have—I should—douse her with words, with vengeance. But I don't. I let a half-grin appear, and nod. "I do," I tell her without letting anger and meanness enter into it. "So what?"

And just like that, I know exactly what to say in my last college essay: "My Greatest Flaw and How It Helps Me."

ℓ

"You're finished?" Dad asks when we're gathered in the kitchen for a celebratory breakfast of crêpes and strawberries—my birthday meal when I was a kid.

"Just in the nick of time." My mother folds a crêpe and hands me orange juice mixed with ginger ale, a faux mimosa. "A faux-mosa, if you will."

"I will," I say and sip. "It's the last time I have to write these kinds of ridiculous essays…"

"What was the one that was tripping you up, anyway?" Dad asks with his mouth full.

I tell them, and help myself to seconds before I head to school. "I gotta go," I say, remembering that today's the day Wendy's handing out the invites to her New Year's bash. I'm guessing that after our semi-bonding, she'll deposit one in my locker.

All along, I thought it was my nose that was the flaw. Turns out I was wrong.

In the hallway, seniors and juniors alike flock to their lockers and search for the thick, silvery invitations. I watch the usual suspects—Jill and her social group—hold theirs in excitement as I slowly turn the lock on my locker. A few lockers away, Leyla reads hers, refusing to look at me while Eddie snags his invitation. He reads it with a shrug and goes over to Leyla. I wonder what they're talking about, but don't have a chance of finding out. Eddie looks over at me. I give him a small wave and he holds up his invite, gesturing to see if I'm heading to the lake, too. I want so much to be able to hang out with him—go running, laugh over tea and crumpets, talk about anything and everything—but it's too hard now. The emails are gone, and so is any hope I had. Leyla was totally correct when she said I had a fantasy life with Eddie—and without it, I'm not sure how to proceed.

The yellow metal clangs open, revealing the few books I have inside my locker. Notebooks, pens, the latest copy of the *Word*, but no silvery envelope. No rectangle of inclusivity. I don't bother looking at Eddie or Leyla or anyone else. I just close the door and head to study hall.

With everyone pretty much mentally on vacation already, the room is boisterous rather than studiously quiet. I take a seat off in the corner near Sarah Jensen, who is busy highlighting her science textbook. I nod hello.

"Cramming," she says, as if I asked.

"For exams?" I slide my bag onto the floor and take out a book, so I can pretend to read while really trying to overhear Eddie's conversation with his friends. Just hearing his voice sends ripples of longing through my body. Why can't the people we are on the computer screen be the people we are in study hall? I think back to some of his letters, the ones I can recall. I wonder if he does the same, if my letters moved him the way his moved me.

"They're not too far off," Sarah says as she chews on her pen.

"Exams aren't until after break!" I can't believe she's so insistent on this. "You've got to let go a little, Sarah," I tell her while pining for Eddie. "Just learn to relax."

Sarah smirks and gives me the same look she gives her opponents in debate. "For your information, I will be relaxing and enjoying myself—at least for part of break. New Year's at Wendy's house, right?" She goes back to studying, leaving me even more alone than I was before. How did Sarah Jensen score an invite when I didn't?

Eddie laughs and claps his hands, a habit he's always had—he does it even while jogging—and I think of telling him to wear mittens to muffle the sound. He catches me looking at him, but doesn't do anything because right then he gets in trouble with the monitor ("Some people actually need to work, Mr. Roxanninoff"), and I have an encounter with Wendy Von Schmedler. She's passing by me and I smell a whiff of a new perfume—probably a "treat" from her mother.

But I don't say that. Instead, in a calm voice, I say, "Wendy?"

She turns around, flanked by her sidekicks and their airbrushed beauty. I could ask her why she didn't invite me. Or I could berate her. But the newfound so-what-about-my-nose? feeling takes over. "Thanks for the invitation," I tell her. "I'd love to come to your party."

Jill Carnegie grimaces. Vienna Thompson actually sticks out her tongue. Wendy just flinches for a second, and we lock eyes like we did on the floor of the Apothecary. "Glad to hear it."

Jill can't take it anymore. "What'd you do, Wendy, send her two invitations? One for her, and one for her nose?"

The room quiets as people wait for my reaction. I can feel it brewing. How easy it would be to sting back as I've done so many times before. How simple. But how flawed. "Actually, I only got one." I point to my face. "We go together—as a package." I wait for Wendy's response. In a movie, she'd be all smiles and hugs and people would cheer as the social barricades fall. But real life isn't like that.

Wendy checks her watch as though she's got somewhere better to be. She can't be too nice or her friends will think she's lost it, but if she's too mean, I'll know she was a fake during our moment of truth in the store. "Of course I invited you, Cyrie," she says, her voice semi-soft. "I left the invite at the *Word* office." Her eyes flick to mine. She really invited me? Jill still looks horrified, and when Wendy sees this she adds a definitive, "Of course, you're only coming in an editorial capacity—I figure you can devote an entire front page to me and the most memorable night of the year."

Jill looks satisfied. Wendy looks pleased. She has her cake and eats it, too. It's not perfect, but it's not bad. I nod to her and a few minutes later, after the bell, head to the office where—sure enough—taped to the door is a silvery envelope addressed to me.

"I'm invited," I say aloud.

"So, I'll see you there?" Linus taps my shoulder. "I heard there's going to be mistletoe."

Linus. Dependable, trustworthy Linus. Linus who wants to be more than friends. Linus who bought my writing help at the auction.

"Yeah—I guess so."

"Did you finish your essays?" he asks, making small talk before our *Word* meeting. I notice that Leyla's not here, nor is Eddie. With a wince, I wonder if they're together, hunched over watery hot cocoa near the ugly sea mural in the cafeteria, or bonding over books. Maybe Leyla is with Josh. I feel reassured thinking this.

"Do you need a ride to Wendy's party?" Linus asks. I shake my head.

"Nah, I'll be fine."

We wait for the others to arrive. Josh rushes in, alone, and all thoughts of Leyla being with him vanish. As if reading my mind, Linus asks, "Where's Leyla?"

Josh shrugs and blows it off. "Who knows. Not like I'm her keeper or anything."

Linus signs to me, *bored of Josh already*. "Did you finish your essays?"

I nod and sign back, *all done, so happy*. My signing is limited, so I can't be super eloquent. "What did you write about?"

Using his hands, he tells me, *I answered a question*. He goes on: *Do you think it's better to risk the truth and fail, or never to try?* With his eyes he asks me to answer that question myself, but all I do is give him the sign that I'm done with signing, that I don't have an answer to that question.

twenty-one

Everything I've ever read or heard about Wendy Von Schmedler's lake house is true. Though the house is built to resemble a log cabin, it's anything but simple. *Neither is friendship*, I think, as I take in my surroundings. Outside the mansion, the lake is frozen and people are skating, and there's a hot chocolate stand, too. As far as friendship goes, who knows what's happening with Leyla.

Out of habit, I checked our old account before coming to the party—just to see if she (or Eddie) had written anything. But she hadn't. And he hadn't—or if he had, it was erased. Then "Dancing on the Ceiling" (possibly one of the worst songs ever) came on the radio, and though it's hilarious in its lameness, I wanted to cry. Leyla and I used to joke about this song. The funny thing is, instead of pushing away all my feelings of missing her, or feeling angry about how things ended, I felt the same kind of longing I feel for Eddie. All my fantasies about how a friendship should be—the closeness, the confiding, the trust, the fun—evaporated, and I wrote her this:

> Leyla—It's me. The real me. The Cyrie you used to sit next to at Word meetings to ask how to spell things. The one who didn't know that Roberto Cavalli was a clothing designer and not a made-up name. The one who wishes she never got involved with the whole email thing. The one who understands why you want me to tell Eddie everything but resents that you took your frustration at your inability to express yourself out on the wrong person. The one who is guilty of doing the exact same thing. The one who still loves "Dancing on the Ceiling" only because it reminds her of you. The Cyrie who misses you and wants to be friends again.

I sent it, but didn't hear back. I don't know if—or when—she'll ever get the message.

I stomp my boots on the mudroom floor in the house's

entryway, and when I take my boots off, my feet are instantly warmed up. Under-floor heating? I look down, impressed. *Radiant heat*, I note on my pad for the *Word*.

"This place rocks!" Josh puts his fist in the air as he shoulders by me.

"It's like old-fashioned hunting lodge meets luxury hotel," I say, writing these thoughts down. Being here in an "editorial capacity" may not be as cool as being here like a regular invitee, but writing articles does have its privileges.

"So, you're just snooping?" Eddie asks me when I've slung my coat down with everyone else's. Tomorrow morning, when people go to leave, they'll have to dig their parkas and hats out from under the piles, but for now the mound of down and gloves grows ever larger.

"I'm allowed to snoop," I tell him, trying to avoid his eyes. Just being near him makes me think of his letters, makes my heart ache in a way that hurts too much to contend with. "I'm too curious—for my own good." I don't explain this, just study the inlaid floors, the gilt-framed oil paintings on the walls.

"Want some help?" He points toward the billiards room. "I could inventory the rooms if you want."

I don't want him to inventory anything or take notes or smile at me. I want him to write to me again. To know that it's me he loved or liked or wanted. "No thanks, I'm cool."

He pauses for a second and then, spying Leyla's arrival,

waves to her. I take off up the stairs before I feel any worse. They've been seen around together recently, and even though I'm glad Leyla's free of Josh yet again, and I want her to be happy, I can't think about her being with Eddie. I can't think of anyone being with him. Maybe not even myself.

$$\ell$$

When I investigate the hot tub area, I find Westies bikini-clad and jovial, splashing and shrieking about someone's lost shorts. I watch as Jill Carnegie is caught under one of the many sprigs of mistletoe Wendy has hung in the doorways. Jill plants a kiss on some freshman who has talked his way into the party, and then suddenly, the whoops and shouts focus on me.

"Your turn, Cyrie!" Jill calls, her voice laced with evil.

I'm all set to defend myself, to stomp off and refuse, but when I see that it's Linus next to me under the kissing leaves, I feel as though I can't decline. At least, not without hurting him.

Ready? he signs. I nod and shrug. He grins. We lean in, our lips connecting briefly as my classmates cheer.

The kiss is fine. The definition of a kiss. Two sets of lips meeting. There's nothing to report that's bad about it, but, I realize, that doesn't make it good. I smile at Linus to let him know I'm okay with it, and he squeezes my hand. I lean on the doorway to make notes about this whole scene, and realize that included in the audience for our kiss was not only Leyla, but Eddie. I put my fingers on my lips and head elsewhere to explore.

ℓ

"So here we have the master bedroom." Wendy points out the features of her palatial house while ogling students take the tour. I take notes about the square footage, the custom-made beds, the extra-wide bathtubs, the granite, the marble, the game rooms, the bar, the chef's kitchen, and the various lounging areas until I need a break.

Groups of kids are clustered by the fireplace making s'mores and laughing. Others dance in the music room where the lights are dimmed and a DJ spins records, and in the kitchen, a professional chef makes appetizers and desserts for a cast of thousands. The kitchen is surrounded on all sides by floor-to-ceiling windows outlined by fake logs. A modern twist on lodge décor. I help myself to an oversized chocolate chip cookie.

"Freshly made vanilla-bean ice cream to go with that?" Clad in a starched white jacket, the chef holds out an example of a cookie sandwich. I make a note in my notebook. When I look up, Leyla is in front of me.

I stare at her. I want to hug her, or make her talk to me,

or plead with her to be my friend. "Gotta love the cookie-wich," is what I say. I put a scoop of vanilla on my cookie. She does the same.

"You look nice," she says. Her first words to me in weeks. *Nice*. But I don't flinch at the word. There's nothing wrong with "nice"—not necessarily. I catch my reflection in the glassy windows. While some revelers are clad in New Year's garb—fancy dresses, starched suits, sparkling sheaths—others are in jeans and fleece. I'm in the latter camp: my favorite worn-in jeans, striped socks, a navy blue cashmere turtleneck (a gift from my parents), and earrings in the form of moons and stars. I fiddle with one now, feeling the star's points on my fingers. In the semi-sheer reflection of the window, my hair is white-blonde, and my familiar profile doesn't trip me up. It just is. *If only I could shave a little off here—a bit there*, I think for a quick second, as my nose stretches across the panes.

I turn back to Leyla. "Thanks."

The music has stopped, and we stand there in silence. Then, from the dance room, it starts up again. We eat our cookies awkwardly, without saying anything, listening to the Bee Gees and Supertramp and, finally, a slow song. I nearly choke on my dessert when I realize—

"I can't believe they're playing this."

"Me, neither," I tell her. "What're the odds?"

Depeche Mode's "Somebody" plays, and the lyrics are barely audible but I mouth them anyway. Somebody. Sumbodee. I look at Leyla. I think about my mother's advice, the advice that helped get items for the auction. Maybe the same rules apply here. Never miss a moment.

"You're a really good person," I tell her. I think about her easygoing manner, her goofiness, her ability to ask for help or admit she's incorrect. "You have a lot to teach me, I think."

Leyla grips her glass of soda and stares out the window at something. I peer to the left, to see what it is.

"Eddie," I say.

"Rox."

We focus on each other. "You don't have to tell him," she says after a minute. "It was stupid of me to want you to do something you're not ready to do."

"That sounds like something I would say."

Leyla nods and picks at her cuticles, then looks at me. "I think I got pissed off at you for being right so much of the time, such an ... editor. This word or that word. Do this, not that. And I wanted to do it back to you." She puts her hands on my shoulders. "And you could! You could totally tell him! I mean, what's the worst that can happen?" She pauses, looking out the window again. "What? You'd tell him how you feel, that you ... "

"Liked him all along?"

Leyla nods. "I mean, I had to be pretty blind not to see that in the first place. But if you'd just told me ... "

My voice is filled with regret. "I should have. I should have. I couldn't risk—" I pause "—losing you."

"But you did anyway." She sighs and looks away.

I stare at her. I've lost her. My only really good friend. "So that's it?" The song continues. Innermost thoughts and intimate details.

Leyla nods. "That's it."

Tears spring to my eyes. Even though I thought it might be like this, actually hearing that it's over is worse. "Oh."

Leyla starts flailing around, her arms waving, her voice jumpy. "Oh. Oh! No. Not like that! Not 'that's it.' I mean, that's it!"

I look at her like she's gone mad. "What?"

The true Leyla comes back. The goofy and funny and sweet one. "It's like drama class, okay? Using different tones to say the same thing. I didn't mean 'that's it' as in forget it. I meant 'that's it,' like let's be friends again. Let's be done with all the … " She blows a raspberry to convey the missing words.

A weight lifts off me, a smile appears on my face. "Seriously? So you got my email?"

Leyla's head shakes, her tousled hair bouncing. "No. I'm also done with emails—for a long time!"

The song ends and one comes on that neither of us knows. "Like it?" I ask, feeling normalcy … if not return, then at least idle nearby.

She shrugs. "You know how it is with new songs—you have to wait and see if they stick with you after they're over." She raises her eyebrows at me. "See? I did that thing you taught me! Talking about one thing when really meaning something else."

I grin. "Well done." I look out the window at the hot chocolate stand, where Eddie is lingering with a few friends. "Think you can do one more thing for me?" Leyla nods. "Take this." I hand her my notebook. "I'm stepping out of my role as editor—at least for tonight."

She watches me watch Eddie through the window. "No more editing?"

I head toward the mudroom for my boots. "We'll see."

e

With my hands cupped around a mug of hot chocolate, I find Eddie sitting on an architect's rendering of a group of rocks. "Mind if I join you?"

"Careful of that pointy one," Eddie advises, thumbing at a rock near my boot. "I nailed my ankle on it getting up here."

On the snow-covered lawn that slopes down toward the frozen lake, Josh and the other sporties play football, yelling every time someone slides on an icy patch.

"Want to play?" Eddie motions toward the game. I

shake my head. I don't want to be that girl anymore, the one who is his platonic sidekick, the one he talks to about all his romantic woes.

"Want some?" I offer some cocoa to him and we sit there, with the stars overhead, while Eddie drinks.

"It's such good cocoa." He pauses, licking his lips. "Is there a difference between hot chocolate and cocoa? Try it, Cyrie."

There's something so intimate about sharing a mug with someone, and I want to, but when I go to drink it I realize—yet again—that I can't quite drink from it without the aid of a straw. "Actually," I say, covering up my embarrassment with facts, "cocoa is from a bean. Hot chocolate is traditionally served with a cup of steamed milk and a pot of melted chocolate. You pour the chocolate in and..." He looks at me with a grin on his beautiful face. "Yeah, there's a difference."

"Is there anything you don't know?" he asks, but I don't answer. We watch people skating, people laughing and rollicking in the snow, and gaze up at the night sky.

"I know something," he starts, and for a second I'm sure he's going to say that what he knows is how he feels. But instead he says, "Do you know there's a group of stars called the butterfly cluster?"

"That's so poetic." I squint, looking at my breath in the cold air, looking at the sky for answers. Even though we said so much to each other online, there's still so much more we don't know.

"Not that I have any actual idea where this cluster might be. There's also the beehive cluster, and the Pleiades."

"The seven sisters," I say. I rub my hands on my cold thighs, feeling the chill work its way into my skin, my face, my bones.

"And the Great Hercules Globular Cluster." Eddie laughs. "But what do we really know about the stars anyway, right? I mean, some scientist could spew out some theory and I'd probably believe it."

"Why, because you don't know any better?" I laugh a little, too. The mug grows cold in my hand and the drink goes untouched.

Eddie looks at me. "No. Because I'd want to believe it."

"Sometimes," I tell him, "I think people believe what they want to just because it makes the whole thing picture-perfect."

Eddie turns to me on the rock, swiveling so that we're face to face. "What do you mean by that?" He searches my eyes for answers, but I stop myself from going on.

"I should go." I can't be in such near-contact with him anymore without being in the precarious position of having my feelings ooze out, spill all over the rocks, and freeze in the loveless air.

"Wait." Eddie half stands up, wriggling a folded piece of

paper from the pocket of his jeans. "I think I do understand what you're saying." He unfolds the paper and looks at it. "This is the best letter I've ever gotten. The best thing I've ever read—at least about me, anyway."

My stomach lurches. He's got an email printout. "Oh yeah?" I try for nonchalance, but I'm dying to know which of my emails really got to him. Which of my words or thoughts he carries around with him.

"It's from Leyla," he explains. He looks at me, his face sad until he asks, "You want to read it?"

More racing pulse, more stomach flips. I switch off my emotions and go into editorial mode. "I don't need to know what . . . .Leyla wrote. Sometimes it's best to let things stay in the past."

Eddie nods. My curiosity piques and I try to see which letter it is, but he keeps it pressed to his lap. "Well that's just it. I want to push all this away, but when I read them it doesn't feel like it's gone. How could something so awesome just disintegrate overnight?"

"Some people think the Grand Canyon was created in a few days—just a big explosion," I tell him with a weakened voice. I'm making that up, too, as an example.

"Really?"

"No." I see his fingers on the page and I can't take it anymore. "Fine. Let me read this incredible tome. Maybe it's just your sports-page perspective."

"Exactly." Eddie breathes a sigh of relief and hands me the paper. "Read it with your editorial eye, and make it seem lame so I can get rid of it." He gives a half-grin.

The sky is dark, the shouts from the football game fading into the background as I read. "*Hey you*—" I pause— "Who starts a letter with hey you?" I swallow nervously and watch Eddie.

He shrugs. "It's just what we did."

"Okay." I keep my voice light, almost monotone, so I don't read emotion into the words. "Moving on: *You're such a thoughtful person, you seem to notice every detail about me down to my shoelaces and the color of the tiles at the diner*— true." I look up. "You are, um, observant, Eddie."

"Keep reading. Go to the part—" he points down the page "—where she says how she feels like . . ."

I scan the page, pretending to search for what he's talking about when I know the words by heart, when I'm perfectly aware of which letter this is—the last one in our frantically paced exchange. " . . . *Ever thought about going someplace far away like Thailand* . . . .no, here it is. *I wish there were a fancy way of saying this, but the truth of it is that I just plain like you. I feel good being around you. I like being next to you or even in the same room as you. In Drama when we're just joking around or at the Word it's almost easy to forget there are other people nearby.*"

I keep reading, my mouth remembering my fingers as

they typed the words to him, my voice strong with the emotions behind it. "*My whole body feels charged up when I'm with you, as though I could run farther, sleep better, laugh more, taste more when I'm with...*" I catch him staring at me and abruptly stop. "Yeah, I see your point, it's a nice letter." My voice falters and my hands shake, not just because I'm cold. I hand the letter back to him.

"Cyrie..." Eddie bites his lower lip and takes time to think about what to say.

Our moment is interrupted by Josh and the rest of the team, who bombard us with their shirtless selves. "Rock on, Rox! It's time for the festivities to really begin!" Josh yanks Eddie's foot and he starts to slide off the rock. "That's right, folks, it's the moment you've all been waiting for—skinny skating! Strip down to your skivvies and skate, then join the rest of us in the hot tub!" Josh puts his fist in the air as though he's leading a revolution. Eddie turns back to me once he's grounded, his eyes asking.

"Rox—come on!"

Eddie laughs, and as I'm about to jump down, I'm greeted by a "hey" from Linus. Eddie sees Linus start to climb up next to me. He pauses long enough to raise his eyebrows at us, maybe wondering what all the mistletoe action was about before, then follows the rest of the sports guys to the lake.

So, you cold enough? Linus signs. He takes off his ski cap and puts it on my head. I sign *thank you* and wonder if this is the moment Linus has been waiting for, our post-mistletoe more-than-friends conversation. "We need to talk, Cyrie."

Oh no. There's nothing worse than letting someone down, than not being able to return their feelings, and I dread saying this to Linus. "Look, Linus, I can't—"

"You have to."

I frown. "Well, don't get pushy. You can't make someone feel—"

Linus shoulders me. "Who said anything about feeling? I bought you. You owe me."

"Oh!" I smile with relief. "The auction. You want me to write something for you. Okay. What is it? Let me guess— you're weaseling out of that school budget meeting and want me to cover it for you."

Linus nods enthusiastically, and then at the same time says, "No." He clears his throat. "I actually need help writing a letter."

My face shows my surprise, my lips turned down and my eyebrows raised. "Like for college?"

He shakes his head. Out on the ice the skinny skaters whoop it up, freezing and acting silly and shouting. "I want you to write a personal letter for me. A love letter." He looks nervous, picking at the lint on his sweater and unable to make eye contact.

"Um…"

"You know you can. Make it sound really great, okay? Like you're writing to the other half of you. The missing pieces and the parts that complement you. How friendship can turn into…"

He wants me to write this. To write for him all the things he can't say to me. "I don't know, Linus, I mean—"

"Cyrie," his voice is stern, serious. "Please. Do this for me, okay?" He touches my shoulder. "I know it's weird." From his back pocket, he pulls out a little notebook, the kind we use at the *Word* to jot notes at meetings or write down quotations for articles. "I'll write. You dictate."

"Fine," I say, "but not out here." I glance at the ice. Even from a distance I can see Eddie sliding. "Let's go inside."

Wendy's house affords nothing if not a chance to escape the cold and the clutter of people. We bypass the game room (the billiard balls clicking together), more mistletoe, and a tipsy Wendy trying to perfect her pout in the hallway mirror.

"Here," Linus pulls me into the breakfast nook in the kitchen. "This is fine."

I slide into the leatherbound booth. "This place looks more like an upscale steakhouse than a family kitchen."

Linus laughs and whips out his pad. "Now start."

I tap my fingers on the table, wishing the wood wasn't

quite so polished. As is, its high-gloss sheen reflects my face from the bottom up, the underside of my beak making me lose my train of thought. "Okay. Start with—'Like the newly budding forsythias in spring, friendship can blossom when you least expect it.'"

Linus tilts his head back and forth, considering. "That's a little fluffy, don't you think?"

I make a face. "I think it's fine. Anyway, then, let's see ... "

"Something about the feeling of being together, about it being the right move." He looks deep into my eyes and I have to look away. I should offer to write a break-up letter instead, for the relationship that's never going to happen. He's an acceptable kisser and a great guy, but—

"Hey, I paid up, keep going." Linus poises his pen to write.

"You never know when love will tap you on the shoulder. Or if it will," I say, and he jots it all down. "But when it does, there's not much you can do to quell the desire."

Linus nods. "This is good!"

He looks happy. How then, can I say what I'm about to say? "The thing is, I can't help you." He writes that down. I reach out and put my palm on the paper so he stops. "No. Don't write that part. What I'm saying is ... " I take a breath that feels ocean-deep, filled with the truth I've been shoving away for so long. "I can't do this, Linus. I'm not the girl for you. I don't feel the way you feel—or, I do, but not with you if that makes sense. I don't want to write a love letter to myself because—" I look at him, but he doesn't look sad. He doesn't look upset, he looks—

"Pathetic." Linus shakes his head, but his voice isn't angry. "You thought this was for you? Why the hell would I buy a letter to have you write to yourself?" As he says this, it does start to feel far-fetched. "Do you think I'm that tongue-tied around you?" My mouth hangs open in shock until I cover it with my hand. "All this time, you thought I wanted to turn our friendship into a ... a thing?"

"A relationship, yeah." I blush, feeling both conceited and dumb at the same time. "I just didn't ... "

"That was mistletoe. Tradition." He smirks. "And this—" he swats at my hand with his pad "—is not for you." He closes the notebook. "It's for ... " He points with his eyes over to the stove, where the hot cider bubbles away. "Her."

The familiar stance. The brown hair flecked with gold. The smiling face.

"Leyla? You like her?" Everyone does. Of course they do.

"So much," Linus says.

I feel the heat creep over my chest, my legs, my face. My nose is probably red from the cold and starting to chafe with the forced-air heat. "Then tell her," I command him. "You don't need my skills for that. You're the one who won that writing award as a freshman."

"That was for science writing."

"So?" I glance at Leyla. She sees us now and starts to come over. "Just write it. Say all the things you think and you can't go wrong." I look at Linus and see him not as the shy boy who signs hello, not as the spine of the *Word*, but as a good-looking guy who kisses well and has all the depth anyone could ask for. "Leyla's lucky. She'd be lucky to be with you." Leyla's nearly here. "You'd be lucky, too."

Without having to say anything, Leyla and I lock eyes and I know everything's cool with us, that our conversation earlier means we'll get back to being what we were. Or maybe better—maybe not what we were, but who we are.

"I gotta get some air," I tell them, and leave Linus and Leyla to figure out whatever they have.

The hallway that leads to the front door is lined with a long mirror. Trimmed in dark oak, the thing extends from one end of the hallway to the other, making it impossible not to see yourself.

"My mother's cruel joke," Wendy says to me from one end as I near the front door.

"Do you ever wonder why she wants you to focus so much on the exterior?" I ask her.

Wendy shrugs. "Because she wishes she was my age still?"

"Maybe." My own reflection is everything I don't want to see. "Or maybe... maybe it's more like if she points to the outside of you, the outside of herself, she doesn't have to bother with the inside parts. The parts that are harder to change."

Wendy doesn't say anything, but I hear my own words for the first time. Staring at my face, my whole self, I know that it's not my nose—but my feelings—that I can't hide. And that a nose job won't change the way I live my life. That altering my honking great beak won't do anything to get rid of the longing I carry inside.

"You can change your looks, but you can't change your heart," Wendy says. Her voice echoes in the empty corridor.

I smile at her. "That's poetic."

"It's from a nail polish ad I read once," she admits. "But true, anyway." She trots off toward the sound of partying.

I face myself again, and I know that what shows most on my face isn't the thing in the center, isn't the feature that I've always thought betrayed me, but the crush that is apparent on every part of me. As I open the front door, everything Leyla said comes back to me—that not saying anything is a lie to myself. A lie to Eddie. A lie that is more blatant than the biggest nose.

I don't realize I'm running until I'm halfway down the long driveway and panting in the cold. Surrounded by snow-topped pines and thickly set woods, I stop and catch my breath. Headlights swivel on the paved drive, and I wave just so they see me. But the car slows down. The driver's side window slides open and Eddie's in the front seat.

"Glad to see you're not partaking in some skinny driving," I say, joking, but my voice has lost its flair. I can't joke anymore. It hurts too much.

"Nope—I'm all clothed. Making a run into town for some much-needed sparklers. How could Wendy forget those? What else are you supposed to do when the clock strikes midnight?" He looks at me and I look away. *You're supposed to kiss someone*, I think. "Wanna come with me? Just a quick run?"

I make one more attempt at being his friend only. His buddy. His sparkler-run, jogging, hanging-out, chitchat buddy. "Sure." I get into the warm car and buckle up as we drive toward town.

Eddie parks in front of Hale's Liquors. "I thought you said we were getting sparklers."

He shrugs. "Yeah. And maybe beer?" He produces an ID from his pocket and hands it to me.

"You have a goatee in this."

"It's my cousin's. Think it'll fly?" He slouches toward the entrance.

"Honestly? No." I follow him inside the brightly lit store. We wander the aisles, trying to feign indifference. Eddie snags a couple of six-packs and a handful of beef jerky, but before we approach the cash register the clerk offers this:

"Hey, guy." He waves to Eddie and studies us. "I'm going to save you the embarrassment of trying to purchase the goods in your hands. I don't want to have to turn you down in front of your girlfriend."

It's my turn to blush. I bolt from the store and Eddie follows, leaving the illegal drinks and chewy meat products behind.

"Hey—Cyrie—wait up!"

I go to the car. "We should head back."

Eddie sticks his tongue out and blows a white burst of breath into the air, and then laughs. "Well, this was successful." He hoists himself on the hood of his car. "Climb on. It's warm."

Reluctantly, I join him. He reaches into his pocket and pulls out a folded paper.

"I think I'm done with that for tonight," I tell him. I'm done with letters. Done with writing and trying to figure it all out.

"Okay, but humor me just one more time. Read this."

The paper he hands me isn't the email I read before. But I do as he asks, and read it aloud. "*Sometimes I wonder what would happen if I pulled down all the walls I've built up and just started fresh. No concrete. No spackling. No paint, even. Just me being me and not worrying about how I look or act or sound.*

Maybe if we all did this then we'd just be able to look our prob-lems—or our loves—in the face and say…" I look up. "It stops there." It stops there because I should complete the thought. Look love in the face and say…what?

Eddie shakes his head. "No, it doesn't. There's a P.S."

I look down and read aloud. "*P.S. Cyrie wrote this. Lets talk. Form, Leyla.*"

"It's not her missing apostrophe that makes me know it's true," Eddie says, pointing to it. "Or that she wrote 'form' instead of 'from.'"

"It's an easy mistake," I say. "She tries to type fast…"

Eddie waits for me to say something more. "That's it?"

I nod. My heart races, my mouth goes dry, my blood pulses. Visions of him at our meetings, at Any Time Now, at the auction, running, laughing in Drama, all come back to me. "Yeah. Leyla's a good typer."

Eddie slides off the car and stands up about a foot from me. "She is a good typer?" he echoes. "Typist, you mean."

Typist. I made a mistake. I did. "I screwed up."

"It's just grammar." Eddie sweeps his hand through his hair and takes a step toward me. I watch his feet bringing him closer, and then force myself to meet his gaze.

"Not with that." I cover my face with my hands and then stop. I look at him head-on. "I…" I start. "I…"

Eddie waits, encouraging me with his eyes the same way

he does every time I'm with him, as though he gets me and is willing to wait to hear what I have to say.

"I wrote the emails." I spit it out, and the words fling themselves into the night air. "I wasn't trying to lie. I didn't want to deceive you but I couldn't tell you myself. And then it got out of hand, and I couldn't just say 'oh excuse me but I'm the one you've been' ... " The heat starts to fade from the car's hood, leaving my body cold and my hands shaking. Eddie listens to me ramble. "And I know that you liked her ... "

"I still do," Eddie says. His voice is kind, serene, unapologetic.

I fight tears and humiliation. "Which is fine."

"Fine? You can't think of a better word than 'fine'?" He grins and it slices through my heart. "I believe the word is 'incredible.' 'Magnificent.' 'Wondrous.'" All the words he wrote in his emails. He steps even closer to me and without explaining more, puts his hands on my face, tilts my head so our noses don't bump—and kisses me, long and hard.

We kiss in the cold air and my body feels as though it has been set ablaze—my heart is thumping, but my mind is blissfully calm.

"But you like *her* ... " I finally say.

"You. I like you. I was speaking in the third person, editor." Eddie cracks up. He touches my hair, pulling it free of its elastic and hugging me. My hair falls over my face and he sweeps it away.

"You already knew?" I pinch myself to know that this is real. Then I see my profile in the harsh parking lot light, and know for sure that it is.

"Not right away. But I figured it out." Eddie sits next to me and I somehow have the courage to sling his arm over my shoulders. "It doesn't take a comparative lit major to notice that the articles Leyla's written for the *Word* aren't exactly similar in tone to the emails."

"But it's plausible..."

Eddie turns so that we're able to see each other. "And then Leyla forwarded this one..." he takes the letter from me.

"I saved it as a draft. Just, you know, one I wouldn't ever send." I could be angry with her for showing it to him, but I can't be. Not now.

Eddie suddenly disappears into his car and I follow, thinking that maybe it's over, this evening, the enchantment—that reality will set in and he'll see my face in all of its disproportionate glory. He turns the interior light on and I fight the urge to flinch. The green tint and overhead angle has never been flattering. Then I think about Wendy, and all the energy she spends on her physical self, and how if I let go of that—the way I did online, the way I did in my correspondence with Eddie—I'd be happier.

"How come you never said anything?" I ask him. Eddie rummages around in the glove compartment.

"Because I didn't want to mess it up." He looks at me

over his shoulder, his body leaning across the seat and into mine as he digs. "I thought it might scare you off."

"Like I'm a horse and I'll buck?"

"Sort of like that, yeah. Here." He holds a stack of papers in his hand. "This is all of them." He hands them to me.

"You don't want them anymore?" I search his face for answers, and then realize he's doing the same to me. He's not looking over my nose, not ignoring it, but incorporating it into everything—as part of me, part of us.

"Don't be ridiculous. I printed everything out at home for myself. These are for you. I know how you are about looking over drafts and editing..."

"I won't edit these." I look at the words, our plethora of witticisms and wonders, our questions and answers. "They're perfect."

"Perfect?" He asks this with his eyes and mouth.

"Not perfect." If it was perfect, I'd never have messed up and wouldn't be sitting here in his car with him, about to reach for his hand. "Nothing's perfect. They're fine."

"Fine?"

I laugh, and Eddie takes my hand. "Better than fine. Magnificent. Wondrous. Incredible. Ineffable."

"Ohhh—SAT word. Good call." He puts his arms around me and pulls me to him. Our mouths meet over the emergency brake and then he whispers, "Prodigious. Phenomenal. Don't forget those."

We kiss, and for once I don't need adjectives to explain how I feel. I don't need a mirror or a shadow to mark my thoughts of happiness. I just need to say it. "I like you so much, Eddie."

"I know," he says. "And for the record, it's mutual."

I nod, and with the hideous parking lot light behind us and the moon's glow in front, we kiss. Our mouths meet, and our minds, and—every now and again—our noses. And we stay like this, kissing, and being exactly the people we were—and are—until this night seeps into the next, new day.

About the Author

Emily Franklin is the author of over a dozen books for teens, including the critically acclaimed seven-book series, The Principles of Love. Other Young Adult titles include *The Other Half of Me*, the Chalet Girls series, and, forthcoming, *The Half-Life of Planets*. Her books for adults include two novels, *The Girls' Almanac* and *Liner Notes*. Her next book, a collection of essays and recipes, is *Too Many Cooks: A Mother's Memoir of Tasting, Testing, and Discovery in the Kitchen*. Visit her at www.emilyfranklin.com.